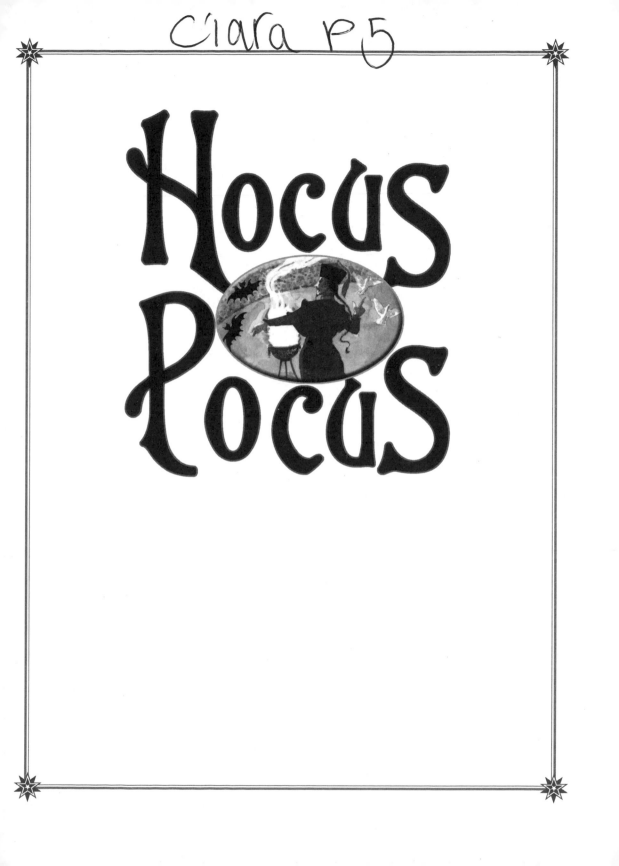

Paul Kieve

Hocus Pocus

A Tale of Magnificent Magicians and Their Amazing Feats

Illustrated by
Peter Bailey

BLOOMSBURY

For my dear sister, Karen, who vanished too soon
but will always be remembered with great love

First published in Great Britain in 2007 by Bloomsbury Publishing Plc
36 Soho Square, London, W1D 3QY

Text copyright © Paul Kieve 2007
Illustrations copyright © Peter Bailey 2007
The moral rights of the author and illustrator have been asserted

Poster images courtesy of The Nielson Poster Collection – Las Vegas, NV, USA
and the author's personal collection

A CIP catalogue record of this book is available from the British Library

ISBN 978 0 7475 9089 7

All papers used by Bloomsbury Publishing are natural, recyclable products
made from wood grown in well-managed forests. The manufacturing processes
conform to the environmental regulations of the country of origin.

Typeset by Dorchester Typesetting Group Ltd
Printed in China by C&C Offset

1 3 5 7 9 10 8 6 4 2

www.bloomsbury.com/hocuspocus

Contents

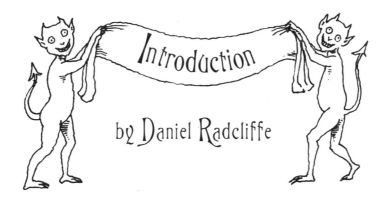

Introduction

by Daniel Radcliffe

For the past few years I have been involved with magic of the movie kind. Playing Harry Potter, I have witnessed amazing feats of cinematic wizardry which leave me breathless. When I see the end result of a scene which I filmed months earlier – complete with special effects – I am in awe of the technical achievements which enable me to have a conversation with Dobby the house elf (previously an orange ball at the end of a stick!) or fly Buckbeak through the glorious Scottish mountains (previously a very cold studio at Leavesden!).

However, when I was filming *Harry Potter and the Prisoner of Azkaban* I met Paul Kieve, who was the magic consultant on the film, and he introduced me to a world of magic that had the same impact on me as the astonishing effects which bring the *Harry Potter* movies to life.

We talked for many hours about magic and I was completely caught up with his passion, energy and belief in his art. I also had the privilege of Paul training me in magic skills over many months. I learned some wonderful illusions, with which I have entertained my friends at parties, on the set and at school! To break the ice with new actors joining the *Harry Potter* films, I often show them some magic – Emma Thompson did actually scream when I first met her and performed an amazing trick which Paul had taught me!

Apart from the practical side, Paul opened my mind to a world which I had previously known nothing about. I quickly became obsessed with it and wanted to know who were the greatest magicians? What are the most difficult illusions to perform? Paul was always there, not only with an answer but with amazing background knowledge. Paul's world of magic is one of beauty and elegance, where a simple performance executed with precision will leave an audience bewildered. How many people can do that?

Step into the pages of *Hocus Pocus* and prepare to be astonished!

Daniel Radcliffe

Hocus Pocus was the title of the first complete book on magic ever written in English. It was a fantastic work which contained lessons on everything from fire breathing to card tricks – skills that would have amazed people when it was first published in 1634. Some of the magic described is still astonishing people today!

My *Hocus Pocus* is very different – it's bang up to date but it's very much inspired by master magicians from days of old.

Within these pages I'll share with you the spellbindingly spooky story of how I came to meet and learn from the greatest magicians who ever lived. You'll hear about their strange lives and mysterious deaths. You'll watch in awe from my bedroom window as one master magician vanishes an elephant in the back garden, while another levitates a lady in my front room. Who would have thought such extraordinary events would happen in an ordinary house in east London?

And the other exciting thing is that you'll receive

magnificent master classes from these great magicians who performed at a time before television. Woven into the story are wonderful magic tricks which you'll be able to try for yourself. And if you turn the pages with care and read very closely, you'll discover the real secrets – hints and tips on how to perform your tricks so that they look really, well, magical!

And when the story is over, I've gathered a miscellany of magical feats for you to learn. By the end you'll be able to step on to the stage, amaze your audience and, before you know it, be on a path to becoming a great magician yourself.

Paul Kieve

Chapter 1

How It All Began

I LOVE MAGIC — I'VE LOVED IT since I was a kid. Mum and Dad gave me a magic set for my tenth birthday, and I can still remember the excitement of unpacking the strange-looking props from the box as if it was yesterday: Chinese bowls decorated with golden dragons which made grains of rice multiply and then transform into water; little balls that appeared, disappeared and multiplied underneath magical cups as if they had a life of their own; and a little square of glass in a red frame — you could push a sharpened pencil right through the glass even though it didn't have a hole in it! Now that was amazing. I was hooked straightaway and was desperate to find out more.

One day, soon afterwards, my dad took me to the British

Museum in London, a pretty mysterious place in itself. But it just so happened that opposite the front entrance to the museum there was the most exciting shop I'd ever seen in my life – a magic shop. Through the cobwebs in the front window I could see more mysterious-looking objects – similar to the props in my magic set but much bigger and older looking. They were made in metal and wood, not plastic and rubber like the ones in my box. I persuaded Dad to take me in.

When I stepped inside – well, I'd never seen anything like it in my life. The place was full of enchanting old apparatus in dusty glass cabinets: silver balls, large metal rings, painted wooden boxes, bunches of flowers made from feathers. In one cabinet was an old wax head of a lady called Mary Maskelyne (it said so on the label). She seemed to be very smiley considering she didn't have a body. I spent all my pocket money on things I could afford, like playing cards and coloured handkerchiefs. But the thing that I really wanted was right at the

back of the shop – a
mysterious-looking
sarcophagus. You
know what I mean?
A kind of human-
shaped mummy case,
only bigger than life-
size. It was decorated
with fantastic images
of Ancient Egyptian
gods in bright orange,
turquoise and what
looked like real gold
leaf. No one was
allowed near it apart
from the fearsome

man behind the counter. What could it be for? Sawing someone in half? Making someone disappear? I would lie awake at
night and imagine that I was a famous magician performing a
big magic show with mystical magical apparatus just like that
weird, wonderful cabinet.

One day, just after the Christmas holidays, when I had more
money saved up than usual (about £7.50), I persuaded Mum
and Dad to take me back there (pretending that I mainly
wanted to go to the museum). I plucked up the courage to ask
the man behind the counter how much the mummy case was.

'More than a few weeks' pocket money for you, son,' he said

rudely, glaring down at me as if I was a silly child. Well, I suppose I was a child, but I wasn't silly.

I'll show him, I thought. *One day . . .*

I was determined to become the best magician I could be. I loved learning to perform magic with playing cards and coins and the small props I'd got from the shop, but then I got more ambitious. I'd seen magicians on TV performing 'grand illusions' – making tigers and aeroplanes disappear. I wanted to be able to do big-scale magic just like that! So when I was in my teens I used to spend hours covering all my school books with sketches of ambitious magical ideas (it beat algebra, I thought) and figuring out how to make my own props. The miserable man in the magic shop didn't put me off. I made a magic cabinet out of boxes from the supermarket, painting it up carefully to look like the one I'd seen. Unfortunately, when I tried to cut my little brother in half (something I'd always wanted to try) he remained firmly in one piece, but the box collapsed into a heap! There's a good reason why these things are usually made out of wood.

I used to practise all the time – I could make a silver ball float in the air, make lit candles

appear and vanish, and I eventually succeeded in cutting my sister, Karen, into three pieces (and putting her back together again, of course). And not many people can say that they have levitated their grandma on a flying carpet! One day, I was sitting on my bed as my mum chatted to me about my school work – and my leg fell off! It gave her quite a shock, but it was just me trying out a new magical idea.

When I left school, I started to work professionally as a magician – and that's what I've done ever since. I've travelled around the world, performing on cruise ships, in theatres and on TV. I've stood in front of 6,000 people at the Royal Albert Hall in London and made someone disappear . . . It's a cool job! Then again I did have a bit of help – kind of spooky help – but I'll tell you about that in a while.

When I'm back in Hackney, East London (where I live), things are a bit different. Life isn't so glamorous, what with the shopping and cooking and washing-up and stuff. And my work is different too. I sometimes get asked to design strange magic effects for theatre plays, like changing children into mice, or teaching an opera singer how to appear out of a grandfather clock! It's quite a puzzle to think of ways of doing these things, but I have to start somewhere – normally with a meeting in the centre of London and to get there I have to take the bus. I've always taken buses around the city and there's a very good reason why. When I first moved into my house, I discovered that on the way back from the bus stop I'd walk past the most magical building on earth.

It springs up out of nowhere as you walk along Mare Street, nestled between ordinary shops and fast-food

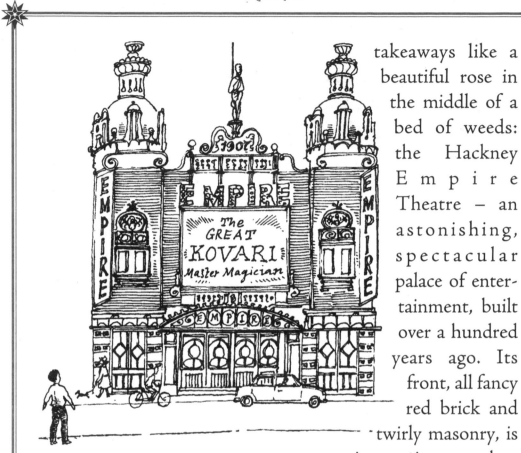

takeaways like a beautiful rose in the middle of a bed of weeds: the Hackney Empire Theatre – an astonishing, spectacular palace of entertainment, built over a hundred years ago. Its front, all fancy red brick and twirly masonry, is impressive enough –

it looks like an exotic temple. But to step inside is truly breathtaking.

The decor is dazzling – with oriental golden domes, ornate columns, stained-glass windows and luxurious-looking red velvet seating. The stage and auditorium seem enormous and much wider than the front of the theatre – like a kind of Tardis (but without the Doctor!). So it seems to be a magical place even before you've seen anything there . . .

And the best thing about it is knowing that the greatest magicians who ever lived appeared there. Houdini, Servais Le

Roy, The Great Lafayette . . . Perhaps their names don't mean anything to you (yet), but they were the greatest stars during the golden age of magic, around a century ago. There used to be lots of grand 'Palaces of Variety' (a fancy way of saying ramshackle old theatres painted up to look impressive), but as cinema gradually took over from live entertainment most were demolished and replaced with blocks of flats and shopping centres. The Hackney Empire was the jewel in the crown of them all when it was first built. It only survived (luckily) by being turned into a bingo hall. Now it has been restored to its former theatrical glory.

In its heyday, huge audiences went to the Empire to watch amazing variety shows, just like we go to the cinema now to watch blockbuster movies. They would see acts like jugglers, performing sea lions, singers, balancing acts – and very often at the end of the show there would be a wonderful magician who would perform impossible things right before the audience's eyes. Women were sawn in half with giant circular saws (with a doctor standing by just in case!). People disappeared from exotic cabinets hanging over the heads of the audience and then reappeared somewhere else. Ladies hovered in mid-air while the magician passed solid hoops around them. Glamorous assistants changed into lions and immaculately dressed magicians pulled endless streams of playing cards and coins out of the air.

And this was long before the special effects we see today in movies and on TV. It all really happened – live! The magician made the impossible seem possible. The great wizards (and the odd wizardess) were very competitive and would do anything they could to make their magic more spectacular than everyone else's. They used elaborate equipment and secret machinery, yes, but they also rehearsed everything carefully, including very tricky sleight of hand (that's magic-speak for using your hands quickly and skilfully to make magic seem to happen). Sometimes they would work on their wacky magical inventions for years before they went before an audience – all to make the most dazzling show possible. They would often argue with each other over who came up with which illusions first, all claiming that they were 'The World's Greatest'.

The top magicians took their acts around the globe, playing to packed theatres. Some made money, too – big money – equivalent to millions of pounds a year today. They were the international rock stars of their time!

When they appeared in towns and cities, their shows were advertised rather like movies are today – with big posters on billboards and stuck on the sides of theatres. Huge, colourful images of the magician in action would be accompanied by tantalising slogans. In those days, audiences were especially attracted by the promise of the exotic and the mysterious – Indian, Chinese or Egyptian costumes and set-tings, great illusions with names that drew on foreign places, like 'The Levitation of Princess Karnak', 'The Shrine of Koomra-Sami', 'The Indian Sword Basket'. The 'Mysterious East' was very popular with Western audiences at the time, with its promise of ancient secrets from faraway lands . . .

This was long before the invention of TV, remember, and very few people travelled abroad. Other countries really were a closed book – that's why they seemed so exotic and mysterious.

I'd always wished I could have been around then to see those sensational shows. I'd walk home from the bus stop and stand outside the Empire Theatre, staring up at the front, imagining the most famous magicians in the world walking in through the stage door. And I always wondered what it must have been like to perform on that stage with thousands of people in the audience.

From the Empire, I'd walk home, daydreaming about my long-departed idols who I'd read about in books. I'd only be jolted back to the present when I had to rummage around in my pocket for the house keys.

✳

My place doesn't look anything special from the outside. It sits at the end of a row of houses on a rather dirty, busy, one-way street, right opposite a big supermarket. The paint is peeling and everything looks a bit tatty. If you peered in through the windows you wouldn't see much – they're always covered on the inside with dusty old blinds.

But if you walked through the door and stepped inside, you'd immediately be in another world – my world. A world dedicated to magic.

The first thing you'd see is an entrance hall lined with posters describing magic shows from a bygone era: 'Walford Bodie – The Man Who Tamed Electricity', 'The Amazing Okito', 'Coming next week – Chung Ling Soo in his Christmas feast of magic!' They're old-fashioned playbills, listing all the acts in a variety show in colourful lettering. So the star magician is splashed across the top, and in progressively smaller type there's the rest of the acts on the bill – everything from jugglers to performing poodles. The very greatest magicians didn't just top the bill – sometimes they were the whole show.

On the right-hand side of my hall, there's a flight of stairs that first goes up to a small landing, then turns right. The back wall above the landing goes up to the top of the house, and it's completely covered by one of those big colourful posters. It's advertising an amazing magician from the 1920s called 'Carter The Great'. Here he stands, a handsome man, beside a mysterious-looking cabinet, surrounded by scary demons and winged creatures. A ghostly figure is emerging from the cabinet. At the bottom of the poster are the words: *Do the Spirits come back? The resounding question of all time.*

Facing him on the hall wall opposite is a little black and white advert of Houdini, the most famous magician of all, staring intensely ahead – this was to promote a book he wrote in 1911. I'd love to have an original Houdini poster in my collection, but they're incredibly rare and valuable. I'm still hoping to stumble across one in a flea market.

Now if you were to take a few steps forward and walk through a doorway, you'd get a big surprise. You'd find yourself in a really big room, which seems to be much wider than the front of the house (a bit like the Hackney Empire!). It's the very back and leads out to the garden through French windows.

I call this room the Poster Room, as the walls are lined with spectacular images of the great illusionists and their magical shows – a dozen or so of all different sizes. Some of my friends find them a bit creepy: with their life-like colours and staring eyes they seem almost, well, alive. Right in the centre of the wall, facing the window and dominating the room, is a giant poster of a very scary-looking man indeed. He's called 'Alexander: The Man Who Knows', and he's wearing gorgeous eastern robes, with a very fine turquoise and burgundy turban on his head. His sharp eyes seem to follow you around the room. I was lucky; most of my posters were given to me by an old magician when I was quite young, along with a few dusty books. He had said to me, 'There's much more to these old things than meets the eye – just like magic itself. Look after them and they'll look after you.' I didn't really know what he meant back then, but I had carefully framed them and hung them up on the walls.

As well as the posters, I keep all kinds of magical apparatus here, like a little glass 'spirit' bell balanced on a magic wand which, a magician would say, rings only when a ghost is near! Then there's a small black wooden box containing a circular disc painted carefully with signs of the Zodiac. You'd never guess that this once adorned the front entrance to the head-quarters of the Magic Circle in London, the most famous magicians' society in the world. My favourite thing, a full-size Ancient Egyptian mummy case, leans against the opposite wall, made of wood and beautifully painted – oh, if only the grumpy man in the magic shop could see me now! (It's very useful for keeping some of my props in, by the way.)

At one end of the room there's a big glass-fronted cabinet with shelves full of old books. Some of them, like *Secrets of Conjuring and Magic*, have fancy gold lettering on their leather bindings. One is firmly locked shut with a brass padlock – *Exclusive Magical Secrets* (no peeking in there!). If you look more closely, you'll see a couple of very old volumes, dating back to the 1600s. Magic has been casting its spell for centuries.

When I was starting out as a professional magician a few years ago, I'd often sit in this room, gazing at the posters, thinking of the old master magicians and their fantastic illusions. What would it have been like to see The Great Lafayette perform with his menagerie of animals? Robert-

Houdin demonstrate his famous mechanical man? Houdini manacled and handcuffed, trying to escape while hanging upside-down in a tank of water? Chung Ling Soo perform his breathtaking bullet-catching trick?

Those great golden days of magic were gone. All I could do was imagine what it was like back then by looking at my old posters and reading about my heroes in books. That way, maybe – just maybe – I could learn to be a great magician myself. But I'd have to do it on my own.

At least, that was what I thought . . .

✳

It all started just over six years ago, the morning after the first show I'd ever performed in a big London hotel. Looking back I'm not so sure it had gone quite as brilliantly as I imagined it had, but I remember feeling very pleased with myself at the time. I was in the Poster Room, sitting on my favourite comfy sofa by the window, talking to a friend on the phone. I suppose I was boasting just a bit . . . 'Yeah, it was great. Brought the house down. The audience loved it! Even the doves behaved themselves – not like the last show where one pooped on my jacket just after it appeared! They want to book me for five more gigs. I'd not even practised that much for it! I reckon some of these old masters could have learned a thing or two from me last night!' I said as I scanned the faces of the magicians around the room.

As I was happily chatting, looking out into the back garden, I began to feel slightly shivery – as if the window was open. I stood up to check, but it was firmly shut. Strange, I thought. I looked around, still nattering to my friend, but couldn't see anything unusual: just the same old Ancient Egyptian mummy case against the wall, the same old dusty cabinets around the room, with their curious contents, and on the table was a copy of *Alice in Wonderland* (one of my favourite stories) that I'd been looking at earlier on – but that hadn't moved from where I'd left it. Everything seemed normal to me (as normal as a room with a mummy case in it can be, anyhow) and yet I felt decidedly uneasy.

'Are you OK?' my friend asked. He must have noticed

something odd in my voice.

'Yes, fine,' I said, not sounding too convinced. I peered hesitantly around the room again.

Suddenly I heard a loud noise behind me. It sounded like something had been thrown forcefully on to the wooden floor. I turned around with a start.

'Look, Dave, I'll call you back later,' I said.

'Are you sure you're OK?' he asked.

'Yes, fine, I just, er, knocked something over.'

I put the phone down, my hands now trembling.

I looked around the walls at the strange figures staring at me from the posters. They seemed more intense somehow. Their features were sharper, the colours were brighter. Then I spotted it. One of my books had fallen off its shelf – that's what had made the noise. I picked it up from the floor, turning it over in my hand to read the spine. *The Life and Mysteries of the Celebrated Dr Q by C. Alexander.* Strange – hadn't I locked that one away in the cabinet?

And as I stood up a really odd thing happened. For a moment I swear I could hear the little spirit bell ringing. Then, as I went to look at it, something cold seemed to press into the back of my neck – almost like a finger – just for a split second, and then it was gone. But there was nothing there to have caused it. It was a horrible feeling and it still gives me goose pimples just thinking about it.

I felt really spooked now. I looked more intensively around the room, under the sofa and behind the piano. I was peering inside one of the cabinets – though I had no idea what I was looking for – when I heard a voice, which spoke with a heavy American accent.

'Think a lot of yourself, don'tcha?'

Eh?

I whirled round, my heart pounding, but couldn't see anyone. Was I hearing things?

The voice came again – even more sarcastic.

'Fine magician *you* are, if you can't tell where a voice is comin' from!'

I looked round the room again, my heart beating faster than ever. *My house is old*, I thought, *but I didn't know it had any ghosts . . .*

'Ghosts!' the voice snapped. 'I'm not a ghost – though if I was, I wouldn't be just ANY ghost! And yeah, I can read your mind!'

What? Read my mind? Surely not . . .

Trembling from head to toe, I stumbled over to one of the posters on the wall – 'Alexander: The Man Who Knows'. As I stared at the picture of the magician in his fancy turban, long, thin fingers holding a crystal ball, I realised the painted eyes were moving, shifting to look at me.

'What?' I croaked, my legs feeling like wobbly jelly and my heart in my throat.

This time I saw the thin lips move. The same voice said irritably, 'Get outta the way.'

I staggered back and fell on to the sofa, goggling, as the

figure of Alexander detached itself from the poster and, with a slight puff of smoke, jumped down on to the carpet. He immediately grew a couple of feet – no, he already had two feet, encased in bright red oriental slippers. I mean he suddenly got taller, much taller than me. He stood in front of me, arms folded, gazing at me imperiously.

'Wha . . . ?' I croaked again.

'Well, fine magician *you* are,' he sneered again. 'Look at you – the minute you see a real magician you fall apart. You look like a goldfish that's jumped outta the bowl.'

Hang on a minute, I felt like saying. *I know I've always wanted to see my heroes, but not like THIS!* I just went on goggling and gasping.

'Well, you haven't got a choice,' Alexander snapped back. 'You'll see us when we want and how we want.'

What?

'The fact is,' he went on, 'we've been watchin' you – and we've made up our minds. We got plans for you.'

'W-we?' I gasped.

He jerked his head at the other posters round the room, and I realised they were all nodding – Devant, Lafayette, Kellar, Robert-Houdin, Chung Ling Soo, Servais Le Roy – all of them.

Another thought sprang into my mind before I could stop it. *Must be the first time they've ever agreed on anything in their lives!*

Alexander coughed. 'Yeah, you may be right,' he said, not so sarky now. Then he drew himself up and struck a dramatic pose, pointing straight at me.

'Like I say, we've been watchin' you, and we agree that you're not a bad little magician – for a beginner.'

Thanks a bunch, I thought. I'd only been doing magic for years, that's all . . . I felt quite indignant, and somehow that helped me to get a grip.

Alexander said sharply, 'You've got a high opinion of yourself, feller. It's about time you realised just how far you've gotta go to catch up with us.'

Another voice broke in, English this time. It came from

David Devant's poster and sounded friendlier than Alexander.

'The thing is,' he said, 'we think it's about time you see us in action, instead of just reading about us in your dusty old books. See just what kind of magic we could really work. There's you boasting about making a dove disappear, while I can make a donkey – the most obstinate animal known to man – vanish in the blink of an eye!'

I was slow catching up. 'See you in action?' I asked. 'You're going to show me your acts?'

'Yeah,' said Alexander. Then he added, 'Some of 'em, any-ways. You'll see what we can do – and then you won't be so fast to boast about your little act!'

'OK . . .' I said, wondering if I'd lost my senses or if I'd actually dozed off and this was all a mad dream. I caught sight of the *Alice* book on my table.

That's it, I thought. I'm like Alice, in a kind of Wonderland (but without the frock and the hairband), surrounded by these master magicians, who are somehow going to get out of their posters and show me their all-time great illusions. OK, I can live with that. I could learn loads from these past masters, especially David Devant – he was meant to be the greatest magician of them all.

'And you'd learn a helluva lot from me too, feller!' Alexander spluttered.

Just then there was a distinct *POP!* sound from one end of the room, by the bookshelves. I glanced over and saw a kind of grey cloud hovering in the air.

'What's that?' I asked.

'Dust,' a voice coughed. 'That's what it is, dust. You should instruct your domestic staff to improve their standards, young man. Or are you waiting for me to write a book about that too?'

What?

The cloud had now turned into a stout little man with a white beard and glasses, wearing an old-fashioned three-piece suit. He was looking at me severely, wagging a finger, looking like everybody's idea of a crusty old professor.

Professor!

Of course, that's it.

'You're Professor Hoffmann!' I exclaimed excitedly. 'I've got all your books!'

Well, if I don't have them all, I have dozens! Mostly about magic – all aspects of it. I was thrilled to meet him – if magicians can step down from their posters, why can't an author materialise from his books? I was getting the hang of this magic thing.

Then Alexander's sharp voice broke in. 'What's he doin' here? He isn't a real magician. What does he know?'

'You know perfectly well, sir, what I know,' the professor

said sharply. 'I am one of the greatest authorities on the theory and practice of magic, and I am here to ensure that this young man realises the true meaning of it.'

'True meaning?' sneered Alexander. 'Greatest authority? You see how far that gets you when you're in front of a crowd at the Glasgow Empire on a wet Wednesday night.'

'Yes,' chimed in another voice. I looked round and realised it was coming from the poster of The Great Lafayette, a stern-faced man with a little dog by his side. 'You just write about it, we *do* it! Get back in your books and leave the real stuff to us! We know what this young man needs to know. Anyway, your last book was on home gymnastics, not magic!'

The other magicians were nodding too, muttering, 'What does he know?' Even the dog yelped.

I turned back to Professor Hoffmann, feeling embarrassed. He may not have performed much on a professional stage, but he made a great study of magic – his book *Modern Magic*, which he wrote in 1876, was the first really great book on the subject written in English. He wrote books on lots of other subjects too – yes, *Home Gymnastics* (and even *Tips for Tricyclists* – now there's an invaluable handbook), but he became famous for his magic books.

He didn't seem bothered by all the rude comments. 'It's just their way, you know,' he said. 'The artistic temperament. And my home gymnastics actually keep me very fit – perhaps you should buy a copy.' He directed his last comment rather scathingly to Leon Bosco, the roly-poly comedian leaning out of my poster of Servais Le Roy's travelling troupe. *Hmm*, I thought, looking at the professor's pot belly, *you can talk*.

Now the professor was leaning towards me, looking serious. 'Young man, you'll find that these conjurors are always going on about how great they are – they are always trying to outdo each other. It's very important that you never forget the true meaning of magic.'

He looked at me enquiringly, one eyebrow raised.

'Um . . .' was all I could manage.

He sighed, and then continued. 'It is not a question of just doing spectacular stunts, making yourself look clever. You should make people believe that a wonderful thing has happened, something that they cannot explain. Remind them about the mysteries of the world. It's not just about showing off and thinking you are important because you have a few secrets!'

This idea seemed to divide the assembled wizards – half were nodding in approval (I noticed David Devant was among them) and the other half were jeering with a chorus of 'Yeah, right!' and 'On your trike!'

Devant's pleasant, friendly voice broke in. 'The professor is right, though. Why did people keep coming to our shows? Because they wanted to see something sensational – something they would never normally see in their everyday lives, yes. But it also gave them the chance to experience wonder – grown-ups don't get the opportunity to do that very often! You can't create that with a few so-called secrets – by simply doing clever tricks! We should hold the attention of our audiences by telling them the most impossible fairy tales – and by persuading them to believe that those stories are true.'

'Yes indeed,' said Professor Hoffmann eagerly. 'It is the task of the magician to bring about a sense of wonder in his audience. The secrets are important, but they are not as important as how you weave them into a story, make the magic more than just a trick. The secrets are not magic on their own.'

He turned back to me. 'And you, young man, you have already learned a lot – I know this, for you have my books! And you can learn more. You can make sure the old traditions are not lost.'

He gave a little bow. 'I shall leave you now. I have said what I wanted to say, and I wish you luck,' he said. 'If you ever need assistance, you know where to find me. In my books.'

There was another *POP!* The figure of Professor Hoffmann seemed to dissolve and flow towards the bookshelves, where it disappeared.

I coughed a little from the dust cloud that was left behind.

As I stood there, trying to take all this in, Alexander spoke again. His voice wasn't so sharp now. 'Well,' he said, towering above me, 'whaddaya say?'

What do I say? The greatest magicians in history are offering to show me their acts? I didn't care where they came from, what laws of physics they must be breaking – I didn't care if it was all in my mind. An offer I couldn't refuse – and I didn't want to.

'It's unbelievable – I mean, of – of course!' I managed to say. Then, looking at Alexander in front of me and the other posters round the room, I added, to make quite sure I understood, 'So, some of you will turn up now and again. Any idea when? Just so I can tidy up before you arrive.'

There was a chortle from Devant. 'If I know my donkey,' he said, 'you'll be tidying up after we leave.'

'You won't know,' said Alexander firmly. 'We'll keep you guessin'. We could appear at any time.'

He paused and fixed his eyes on me. 'In fact,' he added, 'no time like the present!'

Chapter 2

The Man Who Knows

As I stood goggling at Alexander, I could hear mutterings in the room. 'Trust Alexander to push in front . . .' 'Yeah, he can't wait – always wants to be top of the bill . . .'

The Great Lafayette was grumbling. 'These mind-readers are lucky – they don't need many props. I have to carry a trainload of scenic effects and forty-three assistants.'

Alexander took no notice. He just raised his head and intoned, in a spooky deep voice, 'Yes, it is time. Time for a display of crystal seeing, soothsaying and paranormal manifestations . . .'

The other magicians were now silent, but watching Alexander closely. Professional interest, I supposed. One of

them, Kellar, had produced a notebook and pen from somewhere, and looked poised to write. A couple of
scarlet imps were perched on his shoulder. One
of them snatched the pen off him and looked
like he was about to scribble on Kellar's very
bare forehead. The magician grabbed it back
impatiently.

I shook my head – which made it spin even
more. Was all this for real? And was I actually going to see a
magic act from one of the old greats?

By the time I turned back, Alexander was nowhere to be
seen, and his poster frame had changed shape – it had transformed into an arched gateway to an Indian palace. The lights
in my room flickered until just a small glow remained on the
arch. Yes, I really was about to see a performance. I quietly
dragged over a dining chair and sat down, gripping the seat
cushion with excitement.

For a few moments everything went quiet, then . . .

Eerie music started to rise, seemingly from under the sofa. It got louder and louder as white smoke drifted across the floor, gathering at my feet. I peered deep into the archway – where I could just make out two shadowy figures moving towards me. As they stepped into the light I could see they were identical twins – beautiful young women, dressed in glittering, sequinned, dark green gowns and embroidered headbands with ostrich feathers stuck into them. They smiled at me and then gazed into the distance, above my head.

A loud voice seemed to come from thin air.

'Ladies and gentlemen, the Nartell Twins present . . . The Dance of Abbai Radhi Myrai.'

As the unearthly music played, the twins performed a strange dance. Or perhaps it was more of a slow-motion workout: there was a lot of stretching and bending, and poses that looked almost impossible. They must have been really fit. It didn't look remotely like any dance I'd seen before. I was

impressed – I can't even touch my toes. But I did start to wonder what had happened to Alexander.

After a couple of minutes, the girls froze in a contorted pose with their hands turned towards each other. They were on tiptoes with their necks strained forward. They held their position for so long that their smiles began to crack. The music had stopped and the room was awkwardly silent.

I was beginning to feel as uncomfortable as the twins looked, so to break the silence I applauded loudly. In any case, I thought, Alexander probably wasn't used to walking on in silence.

Right on cue, in strode Alexander through the ornate gateway. He was now holding a crystal ball, his robes swirling around him. His exotic turban seemed to have been adjusted a little since I had last seen it.

He stepped forward purposefully, lit by a single spotlight that made his evil-looking eyes more piercing than ever.

The magician stared across the room, into the distance, as

if he was performing in a huge theatre.

'I am Alexander: The Man Who Knows,' he announced in a deep, prophetic voice. 'Appearing before you in the robes of an oriental seer, it is my pleasure to amuse and mystify you with some tests involving the hidden forces of the human mind. These tests may seem to show that I possess abilities that are beyond those of the normal brain. It is my claim that any one of you can do these things if you give them the same amount of study that I have. You have eyes to see and ears to hear, and a mind with which to think. I want you to experience these things for yourself, using your own judgement to draw your own conclusions.

'You, sir!' said the magician, pointing straight at me. I sat up with a jolt.

'I ask you to write on this card any question that you wish to be answered. It may relate to business deals, finance, love, travel, friends or relatives – anything which relates to your life at the moment. When you have finished writing, place your question in the envelope and seal it firmly.'

As he was talking, one of the dancing twins handed me a piece of card, a pencil and a brown envelope that looked very ancient.

Hmm – what to write? I stared at the paper. *Alexander knows all, does he? Well, I'll ask him a tough question.* I thought of something he couldn't possibly know because I didn't know the answer myself yet! I scribbled the question down and sealed it firmly in the envelope, pressing extra hard to make

sure the flap had stuck down properly.

One of the girls smiled at me and took the envelope from my hand. Turning around, she placed it on a dish held up by her sister. Alexander was holding his crystal ball in both hands, gazing into it, breathing deeply. Then he suddenly stood up straight, transferring the ball into one hand and waving his other hand at the dish. He was trembling a lot and had a terrifying expression on his face. The envelope promptly burst into flames. We all watched as the little fire burned right down. Then Alexander blew the ashes into the room.

That's that, then, I thought. *No one can read it now.*

The magician handed his crystal ball to the first twin, and both girls ran back through the archway. A few moments later one of them returned with two small blackboards and a piece of chalk.

'Have you heard of the spirit world?' Alexander intoned. 'Some claim that it is possible to harness the power of those from beyond the grave to assist in answering questions otherwise impossible to answer.'

I knew that in the days of Alexander, many performers claimed to be able to make contact with the dead and receive messages. It was big business back then and attracted a lot of frauds. With clever stage tricks, they managed to swindle gullible people out of lots of money. The thought of it made me quite cross.

'I make no such claims myself,' explained Alexander, 'but offer this to you as a demonstration of the unknown. These slates were bought here in the local town for the price of six-pence. They are unprepared and blank on both sides. I will now clean them –' he looked as if he was about to spit at the slates but stopped and smiled – 'in the sanitary way.' With that, he displayed the little blackboards on both sides and then wiped them with a polishing cloth. They did indeed seem to be well and truly blank.

'I will now place this small piece of white chalk on one slate and sandwich it between the other.' And he did so. The black slates had thick wooden frames which allowed them to be held flat together with the piece of chalk sandwiched between. I could hear it rattling about in the middle as he tipped the slates from side to side.

'I do not wish to remain holding these slates lest you should think I am involved in some kind of jiggery-pokery. If I may now ask someone to step forward to volunteer . . .'

As Alexander's magical associates remained firmly on the walls, I didn't have much choice and stood up hesitantly. Alexander handed me the little blackboards.

'It is now that the forces of the spirit world are called upon to intervene. I will attempt to summon them.' And with that he appeared to go into some sort of a trance, standing there with his eyes shut and swaying backwards and forwards. The sight of such a tall man rocking violently from side to side in my living room made me want to giggle. I bit my lip as he chanted:

'Mmmmmmnnnyyyy, mmmmmmnnnnyyy,

Ssspirits retuurnnn, ssspirits retuurnnn.'

He was projecting his voice very loudly and I was worried the neighbours might wonder what was going on.

His turban was wobbling quite considerably and I wondered if it was going to topple off his head. Fortunately Alexander's movements came to an abrupt halt. His turban stopped a couple of seconds later. He opened one eye and then the other.

'The forces are summoned. Now hold them up in your hands and listen carefully – you may hear the sounds of writing. Do you hear?'

I strained my ears but could hear nothing apart from the distant sound of rumbling. *How curious*, I thought. *What can that be?*

I realised to my embarrassment that it was my stomach – with all the excitement I'd not had any lunch. Not exactly the kind of manifestation Alexander was after.

But then I did start to hear something – an eerie scratching sound coming from inside the slates. The more I strained my ears, the louder and more pronounced the scratching became. The sensation was very odd, and I could swear I felt vibrations in my hand coming from the slates. I felt so uneasy I wanted to drop them. After a few seconds the scratching sounds stopped.

Alexander snatched them off me.

'We shall now see if we have indeed managed to channel the energies of the unknown.'

As Alexander separated the little boards I could see that the once blank surfaces were now covered in odd scrawly writing. I was astonished and more than a little unnerved.

'What strange and uncanny message have the spirits offered you, young man? Often the messages are too horrible to read. I hope they will not cause you any distress. If I may ask you to read the message loudly and clearly . . .'

He offered the slates to me to read. I took them nervously, my hands trembling in anticipation.

My eyes scanned the words on the first slate and I read them out as clearly as I could: '*You will travel to Torremolinos with Wizardtrip Holidays.'*

And on the other slate: *'On 18 August for two weeks.'*

Well!

My question really had been about my future holiday. Of all the questions I was likely to ask, how could Alexander – or anyone – have possibly known? I hadn't been sure about going to Spain – but still, the answer was relevant to my question, and the way the writing had appeared was downright spooky.

I handed the slates back to Alexander with a sigh of relief. It was a baffling performance.

Alexander passed the apparatus to one of the girls and stepped forward to accept my applause. I noticed he didn't bow much – it must have been quite restrictive in the bowing department wearing a turban of that size, I thought.

'That was amazing!' I said, and finally stopped clapping.

Now what? I thought. *Is the show over? Will Alexander and his assistants just go away back to their poster?* I really wanted to make them stay longer – after all, it's not every day a magician from the golden age of magic appears in the living room! Should I offer them something to make them stay? Do materialised magic posters eat and drink?

While I was hesitating, Alexander started speaking in his normal voice. 'Of course, when I have a few more people in the audience, I do a lot more. I usually get the whole audience to write questions on pieces of paper – questions about their lives that they are tryin' to figure out the answers to – and I answer the questions by staring into my crystal ball.

You wouldn't believe some of the stuff I get asked!' he chuckled.

Alexander suddenly seemed more relaxed than before, and I felt more confident. 'Would you like to stay a while?' I asked him. 'I can offer you some tea or coffee and chocolate. Please, sit down. Would the ladies like anything?'

'A coffee would be just great – and the ladies are fine,' said Alexander.

I rushed off into the kitchen to switch the kettle on. I had to take a few moments to catch my breath and convince myself that I hadn't gone completely barking mad. The amazing Alexander had just performed in my house! I stood there with my mouth open – had I really just been visited by the greats of the past? Had the posters really come alive?

The Mystery Man

Alexander truly was a fascinating character. Born Claude Alexander Conlin, he had become one of the most successful performers on the American variety circuit in the

1910s and 1920s. In equivalent terms, he made more money from his live shows than a modern pop star!

Mind you, there was more to him than performing onstage. Apparently Alexander had got involved with a gangster called Soapy Smith during the famous Gold Rush of the 1890s. Soapy had been trying to force Mr Pantages, a theatre owner and friend of Alexander's, to give him a chunk of all his profits from ticket sales. When he refused, Smith had threatened to kill him. Apparently, as a favour to his endangered friend, Alexander killed Soapy Smith. Pantages was eventually to become the owner of the largest chain of variety theatres in the US.

These were strange times in US history and it seems just about possible – it was Pantages who gave Alexander his big break in showbiz, and he later told the *Los Angeles Times*, 'I owe my life to Alexander.'

Whatever the truth, it's known that Alexander carried out various illegal scams, swindling innocent people out of tens of thousands of dollars. (Talk about greedy! He was making a fortune from his stage shows already.) He was once sent to jail for swindling someone, and then faked an illness in order to be released early. As a thank you to the guard who helped him get out, he bought him a huge house. He was a villain all right, but he was also one of the greatest showmen of all time, and crowds flocked to theatres to see him. But to those that worked closely with him, like the Nartell Twins, he was loyal and generous.

Early in his career he presented big-scale illusions, but later on concentrated on his feats of mind-reading and spiritualistic effects, and became famous as The Man Who Knows. None of his performances were *real* mind-reading, of course – in fact he wrote a book explaining all the secrets, called *The Life and Mysteries of the Celebrated Dr Q* – the very book that had leaped from its shelf earlier that morning! People argued about who Dr Q was – but the secrets were almost certainly all out of Alexander's own show. Nevertheless, audiences still insisted on believing he had special powers!

And he was certainly not a man to be kept waiting, I thought, as I poured out his coffee. He had more than once been described as the most dangerous man in show business.

Holding the tray of coffee, bowl of sugar and my finest chocolate biscuits, I walked into the back room and saw Alexander facing away from me. He was fiddling with something under his turban with one hand, and hitting his head with the other. I stepped back towards the hallway – I didn't want him to suspect that I knew his big secret – oh yes, he's not the only Man Who Knows! Alexander

'knew' because he actually had a loudspeaker system under his turban (as you do). He had an assistant hidden in the wings of the theatre who would open the envelopes that were smuggled off the stage and transmit the questions wirelessly to Alexander's ears (a bit like a 1910 Bluetooth headset!). That's why his turban was so bulky. Years ago, very few people would have known that this was even possible.

Some people tried imitating Alexander's fortune-telling (magicians have always copied each others' tricks), but they didn't have such up-to-date equipment. They did hide earphones in turbans, but these needed wires to transmit messages. The wires were threaded through the fortune-teller's elaborate costume and on to the soles of his oriental slippers. He would stand on a rug, on two metal contact points, which connected to electrical wires hidden under the rug. These ran to a room at the side of the stage where the secret assistant would speak into a device similar to a telephone.

When the mystic stood in the right position on the stage, with his feet touching the contact points in the rug, the electric current – along with the messages – could pass along the wires and reach the hidden speakers in the turban. One night, an imitator literally got a very nasty shock when the stage crew secretly linked up the wires to the mains electricity! Another night, a member of the audience placed a baby's milk bottle on the stage and it fell over, flooding the carpet and short-circuiting the wires. There wasn't much mind-reading that night.

After a few moments, I stepped back into the room. Alexander was now sitting at my dining table, his turban neatly back in place.

'Hey, thanks for the coffee,' he said, smiling, but he didn't make any attempt to drink it.

I sat on the edge of my seat, remembering his reputation. But I needn't have worried. He stayed in a good mood.

I relaxed a bit too, and asked him the question I'd been dying to ask ever since he stepped out of the poster.

'Why me?' I asked. 'Why should all these great magicians appear to me and show me their secrets? There's plenty more magicians around these days.' *And quite a few better than me*, I thought.

Alexander gazed at me and grinned. 'Listen to me, feller. Think what you do. Think where you live. Think what's in your house.'

'Er . . .' I mumbled. *I do magic. I live in Hackney. And there are an awful lot of things in my house.*

The old magician grinned again. 'Let me spell it out. You're a magician, right? You've worked hard, your heart's in it. And you live near the Hackney Empire – where most of the greats have trodden the boards – and you know the place as well as you know your own home. And while we're on the subject, your house! Full of so much magic stuff: books, props – and those posters! It's like you're keepin' us alive.'

'But I'm not the only one –' I started to say.

He cut me off. 'Maybe you aren't,' he said, 'but we figure

you'll do for us. We're at home here, we like it — and we wanna help you make it.'

He leaned back in his chair.

'Now,' he said forcefully, making me jump. 'To work! You should learn by watching carefully what we do in our acts, but we're also gonna show you how to do things — special secrets. Now some things you will already know, but we'll tell you anyway.

'So lemme start with the basic rules of magic. Firstly, you should remember that the power of magic is in the secrets. What's the use of doin' a great illusion if you describe how it's done to your audience? It spoils the mystery.'

That's true, I thought, but that was one thing I did know already.

'Second — you gotta practise and practise until you know the illusions inside out. Only then can you concentrate on the presentation. Making it look good for an audience.'

OK — all makes sense so far, I thought.

'Presentation,' Alexander repeated, 'now that's just as important as the secret. You know that slate trick I just performed for you? No, I'm not gonna tell you how it's done — that's one of my own — but I'll tell you this: it's got no more to do with spirits than it has to do with life on Mars. All that stuff I told you was a story to make you interested — now that's presentation — showmanship.'

I nodded, fascinated.

'Now, some of these guys are gonna visit and you're gonna

see some magic that'll make your eyes pop out!' Alexander looked around the room at his framed competitors, who seemed to be smirking.

'When will they visit?' I asked. 'And how many?'

Alexander shook his head. 'Questions, questions,' he said. 'You'll find out in good time. And you'll know when the last of us has visited – you just will. Meanwhile, you should think about what kinda presentation you're gonna give. Funny? Mysterious? Beautiful? You decide, and then work everything towards that idea. Your costume, your patter – y'know, what you say – everything. First, you better decide what you're best at. Look at yourself honestly in the mirror and ask, do I look good doing comedy? Or can I look serious and mysterious without making people laugh in the wrong places?'

I was trying to make mental notes as he was speaking – he knew what he was talking about. If I wanted to be a great magician, I really had to listen carefully.

'That's great, Alexander,' I said. 'But can you teach me something – some mind-reading or something?'

Alexander fixed his piercing eyes on to mine.

'Great magic isn't all about the secrets,' he said. 'You gotta remember what I've said. All of these fellers can teach you secrets, but they're only a small part of the whole caboodle.'

I must have looked a bit down, as he added, 'But there is something I can show you, just so long as you don't perform it in a turban and a cloak – I don't reckon you could carry it off. You're not tall enough. Some magician copied my act in the 1920s and tried to do the whole cloaked mystic thing — but he was too fat to wear robes and looked like a funny old woman.'

'Of course,' I said, happily agreeing. I didn't think I'd be able to pull off the turban and cloak look either. I look silly enough in a baseball cap.

Name That Object

Alexander rose to his feet once again, his tall frame towering above me.

'Lemme start, then, with a wonderful thing, a great inexplicable feat of mind-reading,' he continued. 'I've taken the liberty of doing some research and tried to make this something you could perform today, rather than something I would've performed ninety years ago . . . I would like you to select one of the three objects on this table and I will prove to you that I have predicted the object ahead of time.'

With that, Alexander removed from his pocket a white piece of paper about the size of a long envelope, and, surprisingly, a modern bright yellow highlighter pen.

'I guess this thing is a pen,' he said, 'as it has a kinda nib that writes.'

'It's called a highlighter,' I said, trying to be helpful. He must have nicked it out of my drawer while I was in the kitchen. *That* was Alexander's idea of research!

'That being so,' said Alexander, 'I am using the pen so that this might become the highlight of your day.'

I groaned inwardly.

He went on, 'I have made a prediction which I will reveal to you in a moment. I would like you now to freely select one of the three objects I have placed in a line here – the coffee mug, the sugar or the teaspoon. You may select any one.'

So that's why Alexander had asked for coffee – to get props for his demonstration! That's thinking ahead.

Now it was my turn to think. 'I've chosen,' I said.

Alexander put a hand to his forehead and frowned in concentration. 'If I may now show you, I am about to write on this paper the first words of a prediction,' he said, writing on the white paper using the highlighter pen the words: *You are thinking of* . . . He stopped and looked at me.

'And if you will now reveal your selection?' he asked. 'You'll see in a moment that I have already written the final words of the prediction and cannot change them.'

'The sugar,' I said positively.

With that, Alexander turned over the white paper. It turned out to be the back of an envelope on which were already written the words 'The sugar'.

I was very impressed.

'Great!' I said. I hoped he would teach me how to perform it.

'Now, you know I never normally reveal any of my secrets like this,' he said firmly. 'But I've come a long way and the idea of all of this is to teach you how to become a better magician. So listen – and listen good!'

He smiled. 'Whatever you chose, I would've guessed right,' he said.

I was puzzled.

'If you'd chosen the coffee mug I would've done this,' he said – turning over the flat highlighter pen to reveal a white sticker on the hidden side with the words 'The coffee mug'.

I began to understand. 'And what if I'd selected the teaspoon?'

'Well, in that case, I would've kept the pen with its hidden message facin' the table, and wouldn't have turned over the envelope but opened it instead to reveal . . .'

With that, Alexander ripped open the envelope, keeping it flat to the table so as not to show the words written on the back. From inside he took out a slip of paper with the words *'The teaspoon'* written in highlighter pen.

'The reason I used that funny highlighter pen of yours,' said Alexander, 'was because it has a nice big flat side for me to put a sticker on. You couldn't use an ordinary round pen.'

Alexander explained some more. 'Never perform the same kind of trick twice to the same audience,' he said. 'Part of the secret is the surprise – the audience shouldn't know what the end of the trick is.'

I was already thinking about who I would try out my new mind-reading stunt on. I realised I could use any three objects and still do it the same way.

Just then, Alexander jerked his head up, pressing one hand against the side of his turban. 'What?' he barked.

Who was he speaking to?

Oh, of course. He must be receiving a message through his secret earphones. Who from? I wondered.

'Say what?' He frowned and glanced round the room. Then he grinned and said, 'Sure, why not?'

He realised I'd noticed him pressing the turban to his ear and gave me a knowing look. 'Remember – keep the secrets you've learned from me to yourself,' he said solemnly.

Then he grinned again. 'Trust Lafayette to be on the ball,' he said.

'Lafayette?' I said. 'On the ball?'

'Yeah,' said Alexander. 'I've just heard from him – err – I mean read his mind. He's gonna be the next to pay you a little visit.'

'What?' I gasped. 'When?'

'He didn't say – I mean he didn't think!' said Alexander. And with that he nodded, turned sharply around and strode towards the gateway. The Nartell Twins were waiting for him on either side, facing each other, posing like ballerinas. There was a little puff of smoke in front and in an instant the exotic archway had been replaced by my familiar poster of 'Alexander: The Man Who Knows'.

✴

Well! What a day! I collapsed on to the sofa, trying to get my breath back. I felt my world had turned upside down. Posters coming to life! Magical visitations! Spiritual manifestations! My head was spinning. It's not every day your dreams come true . . .

As I lay on the sofa, my head gradually cleared, and I started to try and think things through calmly.

So, I was some kind of focus for these magicians of old, and they were channelling their energies – their power – through the posters in my room. Or something like that. They would perform their classic routines for me, and – the icing on the cake (or was it the rabbit in the hat?) – would share some of their secrets. How fantastic was that? Now I understood what the old magician had meant when he gave me the posters – how there was more to them than met the eye. Perhaps the old masters had visited him too when he was young.

I'd already learned a lot from Alexander: he really got me thinking about presentation. His whole show, the exotic girl dancers, his elaborate costume – it was all spell-binding. I looked round the room at the posters. Not a sign of life. Showtime was definitely over. For now.

With a start, I suddenly remembered what Alexander had said before he left – Lafayette would be my next visitor! But when? He was meant to be a very particular man. What if it was any minute?

No time to waste – I had to get the place cleaned up. I wanted the house to look its best, so I rolled off the sofa and whizzed round the room, picking up dirty socks, old takeaway containers and anything else that made the place look untidy. By the time I'd finished, the dustbin was full and my recycling crates were overflowing.

What now? I sat back on the sofa in the Poster Room and looked out of the window. With all that had happened today it was still only four o'clock, and the spring evenings were getting longer. I had to go shopping for food – did I dare leave the house? What if Lafayette turned up and I was out?

I sat for quite a while worrying about this. Then it came to me. I was now in a world of magic — well, part of the time. The magic would happen when it happened. Nothing I could do about it.

Right, then. I'd try and live my life as usual, while at the same time expecting the unexpected. No sweat. I could do this.

So I headed out to the supermarket over the road, and concentrated on dinner . . .

Chapter 3

A Wizard Spectacular

M Y HOUSE STAYED UNUSUALLY TIDY for several days, and I remained unnaturally alert. When Lafayette didn't turn up, I began to relax, and the house started to fill up with junk again. I kept looking at Lafayette's image in my Poster Room, practically willing him to come to life.

Reminding myself that things would happen in their own time, I tried to be patient. And anyway, I thought, The Great Lafayette was not the kind of man who would take kindly to being forced to do anything. He was – how can I put this? – not a friendly man. He didn't have much time for the rest of the human race. In fact his best friend was a dog, a little hound called Beauty. That was her in his poster, sitting proudly by his side . . .

The Lion's Share

Lafayette had been given the dog by another magician, The Great Houdini, and she went everywhere with her master. And Lafayette went everywhere! He was hugely successful. His show was spectacular, a dazzling kaleidoscope of lightning-fast costume changes, sensational illusions and cutting-edge lighting effects.

Some of his illusions were like scenes from a play. One of his most celebrated acts, set in an exotic oriental temple, was 'The Lion's Bride', which included the first use of a wild animal in a magic act.

It had taken Lafayette some time to work his way up to the top of the showbiz ladder. He was born in 1871, in Munich, Germany, the son of a silk merchant. He was originally called Sigmund Neuburger (wouldn't look too catchy on a poster, would it?). As a young man he showed a talent for art, and for a while he painted scenery in theatres – good practice for creating colourful effects.

At the age of eighteen he moved to the USA and changed

his name to The Great Lafayette. (He often signed his name 'T. G. Lafayette'.) His act first included sharp-shooting (that's firing a gun very accurately to burst balloons and slice through paper), costume changes, as well as some impersonations. It was while he was trying to build up his career that he met another magician, Houdini, who was also trying to make it big in showbiz. They met in Nashville, Tennessee, where Houdini gave Lafayette the dog who was to mean so much to him.

Lafayette didn't have much success in the States, so in 1900 he moved to Britain – where he would become a huge celebrity, and meet a most bizarre death.

He first made an impact that year by entering the stage of the London Hippodrome in a brand-new motor car – a remarkable sight for the time. This was just like him. He had a keen eye for showmanship and spectacle. He quickly built up his act and became enormously popular – and rich.

His beloved dog went everywhere with him in the most amazing luxury. When the company travelled by train, Beauty had her own compartment in Lafayette's personal carriage.

When Lafayette and Beauty weren't travelling, they lived in London, at 55 Tavistock Square. On the front door was a panel which read: *The more I see of men, the more I love my dog.* Beauty – who wore a gold collar studded with diamonds – was fed a three-course meal at the dinner table, and not only had a dog-sized sofa but her own miniature porcelain bathtub!

It's not surprising that Lafayette lavished so much attention on his dog. He certainly didn't get on with people. He was a loner. His fellow performers disliked him (apart from Houdini). One of them said he was 'eccentric to the point of insanity' and 'unsociable to the point of rudeness'.

'My two best friends...'

Lafayette made no friends within his own company, either. He was a perfectionist who demanded total loyalty and obedience from his staff. Lafayette's personal stationery said it all: it was printed with a picture of Beauty next to a couple of bags of gold, with the caption: *My two best friends*.

Lafayette believed that Beauty brought him good luck. The thought of life without his closest companion was unimaginable for the great magician . . .

But the unthinkable occurred in May 1911, when Lafayette was performing in Edinburgh, at the Empire Palace Theatre. On the first day of the month, Beauty died. The official reason was 'apoplexy' – something going wrong with her brain – but perhaps she just ate too much rich food. Lafayette was heartbroken. In death as in life, the eccentric magician insisted that Beauty was buried in a way that was worthy of his closest companion: in a human graveyard, a very unusual arrangement. Eventually the cemetery in Edinburgh agreed, but only if the famous Lafayette paid £60 for a plot (a lot of money in those days) and promised to be laid to rest there wherever he was in the world when he died.

Beauty was embalmed – preserved – looking like one of the Trafalgar Square lions with her front paws stretched out in front of her. Her body was placed in an oak, silk-lined coffin with a glass lid. As Lafayette wept over his beloved dog, little did he know what fate had in store. Beauty would be alone in the ground for only days rather than years.

It was the evening of 9 May 1911, and Lafayette had just concluded a performance of 'The Lion's Bride'. As the finale of the show, the stage was dressed very elaborately to look like an oriental palace. The large scenic backcloth was dramatically lit by lots of hanging decorative lamps. As the magician was about to take his final bow, an electrical fault caused a central lamp to catch fire. It crashed to the stage and within moments ignited the highly inflammable cushions and scenery around it. Nightmare!

Flames swept up the backcloth. Many in the audience were unsure if this was part of the show, so a quick-thinking member of the orchestra leaped on to the stage to play the national anthem, 'God Save the King' – a signal for the audience to leave the theatre. The move probably saved the lives of many, but cost the musician his life.

The fire spread with deadly speed. The company were panicking amid the flames and heavy smoke. They were un-

familiar with
the escape
routes in the
theatre and
couldn't see
where they
were going as
the power sup-
ply had failed.
In any case,
the safety
doors into the
a u d i t o r i u m

were locked: Lafayette didn't want anyone spying on his
secrets, and they also protected the audience from the real
lion. Wouldn't you know it – only the week before, Lafayette
had reminded his company to keep stage-level safety doors
locked!

When the fire was extinguished, the backstage area had
been destroyed and The Great Lafayette and nine of his company had perished.

The story made international news. When Lafayette's
body was discovered, it was sent to Glasgow to be cremated.
But as the fire crew excavated under the collapsed stage floor,
they found the charred remains of another Lafayette!

This body was wearing valuable rings, which were known
to belong to the real magician. Bizarrely, the body that had

been sent to Glasgow for cremation turned out to be Lafayette's band leader, Charles Richards. When the fire broke out, he was dressed identically to the magician, in his role as a secret double in 'The Lion's Bride' illusion. Lafayette had performed his final illusion after his death!

Eventually, Lafayette was reunited with Beauty. Over 200,000 people lined the streets of Edinburgh to watch the funeral procession – the largest single audience of Lafayette's career. The urn containing his ashes was placed between the embalmed paws of his beloved Beauty. The Great Lafayette was just forty years of age.

After the fire, the Edinburgh Empire was rebuilt, though turned into a bingo hall in the 1960s, like the Hackney Empire. It was reopened as the Edinburgh Festival Theatre in the 1990s and as a tribute to the strange magician and his company a full stage backcloth was painted of Lafayette performing his final routine, 'The Lion's Bride'.

✴

Whenever I caught sight of Lafayette's poster, I'd think about the strange twists in his life and its tragic end. One day, a month or so after my first magical visitation, I was in the Poster Room, lying on the sofa. (I spend a lot of my time like that – you have to rest when you're thinking as hard as I do!) I was quite relaxed by now – I hadn't given up hoping that Lafayette would appear, but I wasn't holding my breath.

This particular day, as I glanced at Lafayette's poster, my mind drifted back to my visit to the grave of Lafayette and Beauty while I had been on holiday in Scotland a couple of years before. I remembered standing by it, thinking about the magician's strange life and even stranger death, how devoted he was to his canine companion, what comfort Beauty must have brought him in his lonely life . . .

'Ow!' I yelled, nearly falling off the sofa. 'Gerroff! Where did you come from?'

A little dog was trying to chew on my ear. She was a very sleek little dog, creamy coloured with shiny fur, a proper pampered pooch. And she was wearing a gold collar studded with diamonds . . .

'Beauty!' I cried.

Looking up at Lafayette's poster, I realised with amazement that his picture had disappeared! Where was he? What was going on?

Just then the dog started yelping excitedly, rushing round the floor chasing her own tail. Then she shot off to the front door, and jumped up at it, whining, pawing at the paintwork.

I followed her, heart beating fast. No mistake about this — and with the house in a mess! Oh well . . .

Someone knocked loudly on the door, making the dog bark more than ever. Beauty was almost hysterical with excitement.

I opened the door cautiously and peered round . . . to see a large man dressed in colourful flowing robes, standing on the

doormat. He leaned towards me – uncomfortably close.

'Laydeeeez and gentel-mennnnnn . . .' he bellowed. 'Allow me to preeesent – Thee Gre-e-eat LAFAYETTE and Company!!'

He stepped aside with a sweep of his arm, and what I could see took my breath away.

Lined up along the path, through the gate and down the street, was a mass of people – men, women and children – all of them dressed in brightly coloured, elaborate costumes. One little person was dressed as a teddy bear. There was a horse too, a magnificent Arabian stallion, and (rather alarmingly) a real lion held on a chain. Two extra-tall men were carrying an old-fashioned sedan chair with an open top, its poles resting on their shoulders. Seated upon it was a thin-lipped man wearing a gold turban, who was staring down at me in a superior way. The dog took one look and bounded down the path, leaping up into the chair and on to the man's lap, going round and round in

circles before collapsing in a heap. The man tenderly stroked the dog, all the time keeping his eyes fixed on me.

'No prizes for guessing who you are,' I said to myself. 'If that's not Lafayette himself, I'm an Ancient Egyptian mummy.'

Meanwhile, chaos was building up in the street. My visitors were trying to keep in some kind of order, but were being pushed around by people trying to get past.

'You'd better all come in,' I yelled, standing back as the whole troupe began to file in, some of them carrying heavy boxes. 'Er – maybe leave the lion outside,' I added.

When the tall men with the sedan chair arrived at the door, they stopped before Lafayette could hit his head on the brickwork and lowered the chair to the ground. Impatiently, the great magician clambered off, still clutching his little dog.

'I trust there will be nothing but the finest fruitcake and excellent savoury nibbles,' he snapped.

'Certainly,' I replied. 'Whatever you like.' I knew I could always pop over to the supermarket.

'Not for me, you fool – for my companion.'

With that, he swept past me, down the hall and into the big room at the back . . . At least, it *was* big before everybody piled in – now there was hardly room to turn round. I squeezed through and saw that Lafayette was already enthroned in the biggest armchair, Beauty on his lap. Some of the people were standing on tiptoe, trying to open the mummy case ('Hey, we could do with one of these,' I heard one of them whisper). Somebody else had been poking around the TV, and suddenly it came on – a football match in glorious colour. The room fell suddenly silent as everybody glared at the screen.

'Hey, how come the movies got so small?' demanded the teddy bear.

'Yeah – and what's with the colour? How do they do that?' asked a man dressed like an oriental sultan.

'And how come we can hear voices?' asked an exotic-looking woman, evidently a princess. 'Where's the piano?'

As the hubbub grew louder, I looked at Lafayette. He definitely wasn't happy that something else was getting all the attention.

Abruptly, he stood up – making sure he placed Beauty carefully on the ground first.

'Enough of this nonsense!' he pronounced, and a large flash of fire erupted out of his right hand, which shut everyone up straightaway.

He glared at me. 'Kindly stop that box doing whatever it is doing.'

I obligingly forced my way through the spectators and turned off the TV. As the sound and picture disappeared, there was a groan. 'I was enjoying that!' said the teddy bear.

Lafayette looked stern. 'To work!' he yelled. Turning to his little dog, he clapped his hands three times. 'Beauty – my oriental shoes!'

The little dog yapped and jumped into one of the large

costume trunks that the assistants had hauled into the room. In a moment, after some growling, she re-emerged, a pair of fancy slippers clasped firmly between her teeth. She hopped over the side of the trunk and made her way to her master (a bit difficult, as the slippers were nearly as big as she was). She dropped them at the feet of Lafayette, who patted her affectionately and gave her the fattest chocolate biscuit that I had ever seen.

'If I may have your attention, lay-deeez and gen-tel-men . . .' Lafayette was speaking in a ridiculously loud voice, as if he was performing in a huge theatre. I tried not to wince as he was making my ears ache.

Lafayette carried on. 'I would like to tell you a story,' he proclaimed. 'The story of a brave prince, a tragic princess and a cruel Persian king.'

As he spoke, something began to happen – something amazing. The walls of my back room seemed to melt away to reveal . . . an oriental palace!

✳

Showtime

It looked like a scene conjured up by Aladdin's genie. Masses of embroidered cushions were scattered on the ground, while rich, colourful carpets lined the walls and elaborate lanterns hung from a silken ceiling. Some smiling ladies were reclining on the cushions, dressed in flowing robes that sparkled in the lamplight. They waved their arms elegantly in the air, in time with the haunting music played by the musicians around them. To one side there was another woman, sitting by herself. She was beautifully dressed in fabulous clothes, but she looked very unhappy.

There was something in the middle of the room – something that I did not like the look of: a large, elaborately decorated cage. And in it a full-grown lion was pacing up and down, making the bars rattle noisily.

Uh-oh, I thought. *I hope he feeds the lion as well as his dog!*

Suddenly the stage was full of people – drummers, swordsmen and, finally, the Persian king. 'He is Alep Aseem,'

Lafayette explained, by now sitting in a grandly decorated chair. 'His servants have captured a beautiful princess who was shipwrecked in the Persian Gulf and washed ashore. The king has become enchanted by the princess's beauty and asks her to marry him, but she refuses. In a rage, he decides to force her to be his bride against her will.

'The truth is that she had been betrothed to a prince at home. He now hears of her peril and has ridden on his fine Arabian steed to the kingdom, to try and save his beloved from a fate worse than death.'

Arabian steed! I wasn't sure about the idea of clearing up after a horse in the house, but as it was Lafayette I decided not to object. I could always put it on the garden.

At this point Lafayette carefully slipped on his oriental shoes and took the role of the prince, stepping on to the stage. After a lot of very dramatic gestures and some strange dancing, Lafayette knelt at the feet of Alep Aseem and pleaded, 'Please let my betrothed go free, I beg of you.'

The king became angry – so angry that he sent the prince away. 'Get out of here! If I see you again I will cut your head off with one swoop of my sword!' he shouted. The prince left quickly – who could blame him? I had to remind myself that the prince was really Lafayette – I was that hooked already.

Then the king turned to the princess and said, 'You can either become my wife – or be thrown to the lion!'

The princess seemed to prefer the option that would be over the quickest! 'I would prefer death to disgrace and will never marry you,' she said passionately. 'You ugly evil king – you can have your entire kingdom but you will never have me!'

This did not make the king very happy. He ordered his servants to lock her in a small cage beside the lion, and swept away with his courtiers. Just one slave, a tall, burly man, remained to guard the princess.

What was going to happen? I'd forgotten that the whole drama was being acted out in my own room.

I bit my nails in suspense for a few moments; until the prince crept silently back on to the stage. 'Go on, T. G.,' I muttered to myself (feeling in the heat of the moment that we were on first-name terms). 'You can do it!' But no sooner had the prince reappeared than he was confronted by the guard.

They had a most dramatic sword fight – T. G. leaped around the stage, swinging his blade menacingly before he finally slew the guard. At one point I was convinced he was going to slash my curtains down, but he missed them by a hair's breadth. It all looked terribly realistic – but I could see that the slave's eyes were blinking a bit and he was breathing rather a lot for a dead person!

The prince freed the princess and sent her away on his horse – I had to let her out through my double doors into the back garden. Then he quickly dressed up as the princess, wrapping her cloak around himself, and took her place in the cage. All this while, the lion – a real one, remember, with real teeth! – had been pacing up and down, growling now and then.

Now Alep Aseem returned with his servants and angrily wrenched open the door of the princess's cage. He grabbed who he thought was the princess (really T. G.) and threw 'her' into the lion's cage.

My heart was in my mouth – what was going to become of The Great Lafayette? How well trained was the lion? I felt like shouting out, 'You'll be OK. I know you die in a fire!' – but I bit my lip.

The lion paced up and down, staring at its victim and licking its lips. Lafayette didn't make a particularly convincing princess, I thought, but then in the old days the stage lights would have been dimmer.

The band members either side of the stage were now

playing dramatic music, with loud menacing drumbeats. Just as the suspense was getting too much to bear, the lion reared up on its hind legs and froze in position. Its paws

went up to its head – and took it off! It was a dummy head. It was no longer a lion – but The Great Lafayette!

I gasped in astonishment and looked for the princess and the real lion – but they'd disappeared!

For a moment, there was complete silence. Nobody moved. Then Lafayette stepped forward and bowed, and I clapped loudly. It really was the most amazing thing I'd ever seen anywhere – let alone in my own house. I realised now why he used to pack theatres out.

I looked around, and some of the other magicians on their posters seemed fairly impressed. Devant was applauding (well, he was always generous to other magicians). Not Kellar, though – he seemed to be scribbling on a piece of paper, his imps looking over his shoulder. I could see Lafayette had spotted this and was glaring at him out of the corner of his eye. But he was still in the middle of a very elaborate bow, flinging his arms up dramatically and bending very deeply from the waist. What a showman – milking applause for all it's worth.

No sooner had Lafayette taken his final bow than he stormed up to the poster of Kellar and reached into it, grabbing a large pad filled with scribbled notes. 'Thief!' he yelled at Kellar. 'You think of your own ideas yourself, you – you – you pilfering rascal!'

He marched towards me, sweeping past his numerous assistants, his long oriental robe creating quite a bit of turbulence.

'That man is always watching my shows and trying to take my ideas,' he complained. 'He sat and watched my show every night for two weeks just to see how I could catch pigeons out of the air in a net!'

'And did he find out?' I ventured to ask.

'Well, yes – in fact, when he finally performed it he greatly improved the trick, so I went and watched him and pinched all the improvements,' said Lafayette, with obvious satisfaction.

I was still completely flummoxed by what I'd seen.

'That was mind-blowing!' I said. He looked puzzled, so I added, 'It was breathtaking! How did you do it? Where on earth is the lion? I mean, I could see it was a real lion, and you were on stage with it, and the princess, and you became the lion and –'

'Welcome to the world of Grand Illusion,' Lafayette interrupted.

After his great performance, he seemed to be relaxing a bit, looking more human.

'I won't give anything away about "The Lion's Bride",' he said, 'but as part of your education I will show you something, a piece of magic which is just as amazing in its own way. Mind you, you won't need lots of assistants, a lion and a horse – just some newspaper and a pair of scissors. So much easier to carry about . . .'

I could only agree.

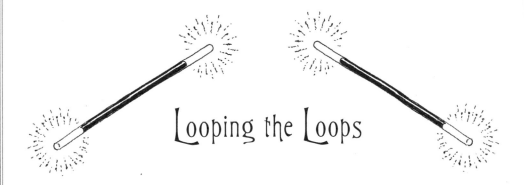

Looping the Loops

The Poster Room was its old self again – the oriental palace had disappeared, and Lafayette had banished his company back into the poster. They'd been making a real nuisance of themselves, turning the TV on and off, trying to get the back open and look inside – and at least one had been hypnotised by the screensaver on my computer and had to be splashed with cold water.

Just Beauty remained with her master, curled up at his feet and gazing adoringly at him (though for all I knew, that look meant 'More food!'). The magicians on the posters were show-ing little sign of life, though Kellar was obviously keeping an eye out – just in case he could pinch anything else, no doubt.

Lafayette started by telling a story. Now, I know this is a good way to get an audience's attention.

'Many years ago,' Lafayette intoned, 'when the world was young, there was an ancient wizard. He used to perform an amazing illusion with three plants, called hula plants. These grew into the shape of a hoop, and the wizard could make them do what he wanted . . .

'Well, you don't get many hula plants these days, so I'll be using pieces of paper instead.'

He showed me three big loops made of newspaper. They looked identical. He then took a pair of scissors from some-where within his robe, and showed them to me. Just an ordinary pair of scissors.

He picked up one loop of paper and said, 'I will now cut the paper loop in half – not across the width, but along the entire length of it. What do you think will happen when I've cut it all the way round?'

He finished cutting, and the paper – well, it fell into two separate loops. No surprises there. Lafayette smiled mysteri-ously and said, 'Having shown what happens in the ordinary world, the ancient wizard now shows what happens in the world of magic. As he cuts the paper, he chants a magic incantation . . .'

Lafayette picked up one of the original hoops of paper,

then cut it in exactly the same way as before – only this time, solemnly chanting a spell.

'Hula hula hula hoop
    Loopy loopy loopy loop
Have some fun
    Grow as one
Loopy loopy loopy loop.'

I felt the urge to giggle at this nonsense, but managed to keep a straight face.

As Lafayette finished cutting the paper, he held it up – and now it was not two separate loops but one very large loop, twice the size it was before. Astonishing!

'And now I will make the final cut,' he said solemnly, 'again with the power of an ancient spell.'

He lifted up the third piece of paper and started to cut around it just as before, this time intoning:

> 'Hula hula hula hoop
> Loopy loopy loopy loop
> Wriggle and tangle
> Mingle and mangle
> Loopy loopy loopy loop.'

This time I couldn't help laughing out loud – but quickly pretended it was a cough when Lafayette glared at me.

Finally – 'Hocus Pocus!' Lafayette shouted and, as he made the final snip, the paper fell not into two separate loops, not into one very large loop, but two loops linked together. The Lafayette Bands – stunning!

Lafayette then explained the way to do the trick. His secret was in preparing the three newspaper loops in a special way.

'Careful preparation! One of the golden rules of magic!'

He stroked his Persian beard, which was now slightly detaching at the sides. 'For this amazing feat of leg-erdemain, get me a large sheet of news-paper, a pair of scissors, a roll of sticky tape and a large porcupine.'

'Leger–de-what?' I asked, rummaging in my desk drawer. I was pretty sure I had the newspaper, the scissors and some sticky stuff, but a por-cupine? I did have a pineapple in the kitchen – would that do?

'Legerdemain,' said Lafayette grandly. 'Sleight of hand in French. And by the way,' he added, 'I was joking about the porcupine.'

For the first time that evening, Lafayette laughed. His face seemed to crack, and he sounded a bit like a toad croaking but at a higher pitch. As he chuckled a large chunk of solidified stage make-up fell off his forehead and landed on the table. He swept it away nonchalantly.

When I'd collected what he wanted, he said, 'Now I want you to follow my instructions very carefully. First, take a big double sheet of newspaper and cut three long strips from it, all as long as possible and all around three inches wide.'

'That's about seven centimetres,' I said, fishing out a ruler from my desk drawer.

Lafayette glared at me. 'Imperial is good enough for me,' he snapped. Why was I not surprised?

He went on with his instructions. 'Now for the secret preparation. You are going to make three loops of newspaper, but each one of them is a little different.

'First, prepare three bits of sticky tape that are a bit wider than the narrow side of the paper (about 4 inches) and leave them stuck to the table (it'll make it easier in a moment unless you have more than two hands). Take the first strip of paper, form it into a loop, and stick the two ends together across the width with one of your prepared bits of tape. Fold any excess tape neatly underneath each side. Don't do anything special, just make a simple loop. Put that to one side.'

I carefully followed what Lafayette said and eagerly awaited his next instructions.

'Now take the second piece and bring the two ends together, but do something different this time. Before you stick them together, twist one end of the paper once – a half turn. Then, as before, tape the flat ends together all the way around across the width with your second prepared bit of tape. This loop will have a half twist in it.

'Now take the third piece of paper. Do the same as the last one, except this time, twist one end of the paper twice – a full turn – before sticking the ends together right the way across the width. This loop will therefore have a full twist in it.'

As I finished sticking the ends together, Lafayette nodded his head approvingly. 'Now you have done your secret preparation,' he said. 'This is a very good piece of magic – it's actually scientific. There are no clever moves or sleight of hand to worry about. All you have to do is concentrate on not cutting your fingers with the scissors, and telling the audience a magical story to go with it.'

And saying crazy spells, I thought.

Lafayette was speaking again. 'Now take the first loop of newspaper you prepared, and carefully push the point of the scissors into the paper halfway across and start to cut all the way around the loop – the long way. Go all the way around, being careful to keep the scissors near the centre of the paper. At the end – what happens? Nothing unexpected – the loop falls into two loops of half the original width.

'Nothing magical about that – but you explain to your audience that the paper was not properly enchanted. Now take the next loop, the one that you have secretly prepared with the single twist. Go through exactly the same procedure with the scissors – and when you get to the end, go very slowly as you make the last snip. The paper becomes one big hoop of twice the size!

'The wonders of science,' Lafayette proclaimed. 'Now take the last loop (the one with the double twist) and go through exactly the same process – and as you make the last snip something really surprising happens. The loop falls not into two separate loops, or one big loop – but two loops linked together.'

I followed Lafayette's instructions – and sure enough the magic worked for me too. I was very excited and couldn't wait to try it out in my next show – after a bit of practice, of course. In fact the magic will work for anyone who knows about the secret preparation.

Just as I was thanking him, rather surprised by his generosity (what with his mean reputation), I felt a nip at the back of my leg and heard a high-pitched yapping sound. It was that blasted dog again, Beauty, wanting attention no doubt.

Lafayette looked down. For a while he had been distracted by the only thing he loved more than Beauty – the joy of performing magic! 'Feeding time,' he said. 'I have been here long enough,' he added, swirling around in his cloak.

Lafayette's face had turned back into the thin-lipped misery I recognised from before.

'The more I see of you, the more I love my dog,' he snapped. And with that he performed a dramatic pirouette. His clothes billowed out at the sides as he spun and smoke started to appear by his feet and rise upwards. Before I knew what was happening, all that was left was the smoke.

I gazed around the room – the only evidence of Lafayette's visit was the newspaper loops on my table and a half-eaten chocolate biscuit which Beauty had left on the floor. I looked up and there he was back in the poster, peering down at me with his beloved dog by his side.

Chapter 4

Monarchs of Magic

WHAT AN EXPERIENCE! LAFAYETTE'S VISIT was like having the circus come to town in my own home (which it had, in a way). After he and Beauty were gone, I wandered into the back garden, reliving that stunning performance, my head in the clouds. And my foot on – yuck! The horse had left his calling card on the grass.

When I finished clearing up, I was exhausted and collapsed on the sofa in the Poster Room. I looked round the walls – who would visit me next? How long would this go on for? Alexander had said I'd know all in good time . . .

Well, I'd learned that there was no point hanging about on tenterhooks, expecting a magical visitation. Just get on with life – and work. This meant going upstairs to my office and sitting down at my desk, in front of my computer: bills to pay, emails about upcoming jobs to send and, worst of all, accounts – adding up receipts and working out how much I'd spent on magic props and things and seeing how much tax I'd have to pay. I often think I'd rather try and teach a centipede to tap dance than do my accounts.

One summer day, my accountant had phoned me for the eighth time to tell me that if I didn't get the paperwork to him by the end of the week I'd be locked in the vault of the bank for ever. Well, he didn't exactly say that but it sounded quite worrying. His threat must have worked as I'd finally settled down to do it. I stared out of my window at the uninspiring flat roof of the supermarket opposite and the housing estate beyond. I gazed at the piles of receipts with a feeling of deep dread, sharpened my pencil and opened my accounts book . . .

CRASH! Suddenly it was as if my entire kitchen cupboard full of crockery had cascaded off the wall.

'What the –' I shouted out loud, opening the office door and running down the stairs to the kitchen.

But I didn't get that far – in fact, I didn't even get to the bottom of the stairs – before I saw the mess. Scattered across the wooden floor of my hall was a trail of broken plates, teacups and glasses. A large round silver tray was still spinning in ever-decreasing circles – its clattering now the only sound to be heard.

When it had finally rattled itself to a stop, I heard an American accent coming from the other end of the hallway. 'I

am very sorry, sir.'

A portly man with a dark beard was sitting upright on the floor, his face highlighted with heavy stage make-up and wearing a puzzled expression.

The man continued. 'I was just trying to practise my trip and . . . I got everything ready and . . . and – I wasn't trying to drop the tray, really. Mr Le Roy asked me to wait in the wings and run on as a distraction if he got into trouble with his new levitation illusion. And now . . . now I have to get it all set up again and I don't want to be l-l-late.' And with that, he started to wail in a ridiculous way, tears squirting out of his eyes like water jets from a car windscreen washer. He rubbed them with both hands in a very theatrical way.

'It's OK,' I said. 'Don't worry, I'll get a brush and dustpan.'

'No – no,' he yelled. 'Don't get the Russian dustman!' and cried even more.

I groaned at the awful joke. This could only be Leon Bosco, the comedian from the famous troupe of the Belgian illusionist Servais Le Roy. I recognised him from my poster.

'But at least I didn't drop the pan,' he said, seeming a little chirpier, although oddly, tears were still running down his face. He was now holding a large copper pot in front of him. He clapped a lid on and whisked it away again – to reveal two ducks, which hopped out on to the floor, quacking loudly, neatly avoiding the broken crockery and heading for the back room at full waddle.

'Mr Bosco,' I said firmly. The large man stopped crying instantly, as if someone had turned off a tap.

'Perhaps,' I said, 'you could tell me how you got here?'

'You know my name?' he asked.

'Yes,' I said, 'you are very famous – I even have posters of you in my living room.' I thought he would appreciate the compliment.

He did. It cheered Mr Bosco no end and he sprang up with a real bounce in his step. 'Yippee dippy!' he said. 'I'm famous. *Famous!*' he added in a silly voice.

Then he pulled himself together and looked serious. He picked up his tray and put a couple of unbroken glasses on it. 'Come this way,' he murmured, and led me into the Poster Room, placing the tray on the dining table. The room looked perfectly normal to me, apart from the two ducks, which had comfortably nestled on to my sofa.

Bosco gestured towards the poster of Servais Le Roy performing his famous levitation. 'Look through there,' said Bosco.

As I got closer I realised that although the frame was still on the wall, the picture itself had vanished. What I could see now seemed to be a kind of window, an opening. To what?

Astonished, I peered through. It was like looking through a window into another world.

I blinked at the sight before me, unable to quite believe my own eyes. I looked up at ornately decorated oriental columns, plush red seats and golden decorations – and realised I was peering into an old-fashioned theatre that looked oddly familiar. This was none other than the Hackney Empire!

But it wasn't quite like I had ever seen it before. As I gazed across the back of the seats towards the stage, I noticed it seemed far more packed than a modern theatre would be (people seemed to be wedged into all corners), and the audience were wearing very old-fashioned clothes. They were completely transfixed by a man performing on stage. He sported an impressive moustache and was dressed in an elegant red coat, black half-length trousers, very long black socks (almost like stockings) and a crisp white shirt. (Wouldn't get away with that half-trouser look nowadays, I thought – you'd look like a hobbit!) He was holding a large cone of paper in his right hand, from which hundreds of flower blossoms seemed to be tumbling into an upturned umbrella on the stage. The act was obviously just finishing, as the pile of flowers was enormous – much bigger than could have ever fitted in the cone. He took a bow and gestured to the side of the stage.

From the wings stepped a beautiful lady, a little taller than Le Roy, dressed in a full-length, dark blue, beaded dress and wearing a shimmering diamond headband in her hair. She walked to the front of the stage as a set of burgundy velvet curtains closed behind her, and looked out across the audience with a radiant smile, standing in a single spotlight.

'That is Mercedes Talma, Mr Le Roy's wife,' Bosco whispered into my ear excitedly. 'The Queen of Coins.' I watched the stage with great anticipation!

The lady showed both hands empty and then reached into the air. Seemingly from nowhere a large silver coin appeared, glinting in the light. Then another, then another. In front of her was a tall stand made of glass. As she dropped each successive coin into the glass receptacle, it trickled down a series of rungs, making a delightful tinkling sound. The coins were produced in such profusion that they created a shower of glistening light as they cascaded down the shelves of the glass ladder. Talma then reached her empty right hand into the air

and opened her fingers to reveal a single coin delicately balanced on each upturned fingertip. She dropped them into the crystal tower, followed by more and more. After producing seemingly endless handfuls of coins, the lady took a deep bow. The audience applauded enthusiastically and I joined in. Bosco looked at me and smiled.

'She's awesome, isn't she?' he said. I nodded in agreement.

I knew that Talma was unusual in being a lady magician in the age of variety entertainment. It was especially rare for a woman to perform sleight of hand. Houdini himself had described her as 'the greatest sleight-of-hand performer that ever lived'.

Le Roy stepped forward from the wings and stood in the centre of the stage. He looked at the lady with great pride and love.

When the applause died down, Talma swept off into the wings and Le Roy faced the audience. 'And now,' he intoned in a thick Belgian accent, 'I am proud to present – The Garden of Sleep.'

He gestured behind him and the curtains swept open to reveal an elegant stage setting, in the centre of which was a long thin table with curvy legs.

'Here it is,' whispered Bosco. 'The new levitation!' He grabbed his tray off the table and stood there expectantly.

Le Roy gestured to the wings and Talma re-entered. She reclined on the table and Le Roy passed his hand slowly over her face. Talma's eyes looked drowsy and she seemed to fall into a trance. Two assistants now entered with a white silk cloth, draping it over the elegant lady.

The atmosphere was electric as the audience watched the curious events onstage. The suspense was only broken for me by the occasional quacking of the ducks, which were now waddling around the living room. I hoped the sounds wouldn't travel into the auditorium. But even they seemed to quieten down a bit, silenced by the eerie music now playing from the orchestra pit.

'Rise, Talma, rise,' Le Roy chanted in a faintly French accent. As he gently waved his hands over Talma's reclining body, the shape slowly lifted into the air under the cloth. The thin table she had been resting on glided gently away. She was now hovering just above Le Roy's head and he gestured towards the side of the stage. An assistant stepped on and handed the magician a large hoop.

Le Roy dramatically held the hoop out in front of him. Slowly he passed it over the hovering white figure, gliding it from the shrouded feet to the head of the hovering form. It sent shivers down my spine – it was really quite spooky. There didn't seem to be any possible way that Talma could be reclining in space.

'There she lies in ze air,' Le Roy said. 'And there she would remain, should I desire, for all eternity!'

The audience began to applaud, but the magician stopped them in their tracks, holding up his right hand in a commanding way. He stepped towards the floating figure and

took hold of a corner of the cloth, pausing for a moment before pulling it slowly downwards. The silk cover started to slide off Talma, and as it did so she seemed to melt into the air in front of my eyes. By the time it had fallen to the stage, Talma had vanished completely!

'That was amazing,' I said to Bosco.

Bosco wiped a little tear from the corner of his eye. 'It is the first time Mr Le Roy has ever performed that. He has worked on it for so long.'

He put his tray of glasses down, saying, 'I am so relieved that he didn't need me.'

'Well, it did seem to go off perfectly,' I said.

'He calls the illusion "Asrah",' Bosco added.

'It's a spellbinding illusion,' I muttered in awe. 'Servais Le Roy and Talma are my heroes. Do you think I might get a chance to meet them?'

Bosco told me to turn my back and face the opposite wall. 'Mr Le Roy doesn't like anyone to see his secrets,' he said. 'But he's a kind man and likes to help people who are really keen. Wait a moment and I'll see what I can do.'

I turned around, peering out into the garden (which was looking rather overgrown) and thought about who I had just seen.

*

Master of Invention

Servais Le Roy is one of the greatest performers and inventors of magic of all time. He was born in Belgium in 1865, but by the age of ten had moved to London and was already working – as a pageboy (can you imagine going out to work at ten years old?). As a teenager he discovered a place called Maskelyne and Cooke's Egyptian Hall magic theatre in Piccadilly, where all the greatest magicians in the world appeared – and Le Roy watched many of them. Young Servais was hooked. By the age of twenty-one he had been booked for his first contract at the Royal Aquarium in Westminster (they had magic shows there, not many fish).

One of his feature acts was called 'The Miser's Dream' – where he apparently pulled hundreds of coins from the ears of people sitting in the audience. He later taught this skill to his wife, Talma. He invented an amazing act called 'The Flying Visit' where he and his wife vanished and reappeared in boxes scattered around the stage, and finally appeared at the back of the audience. For one of his acts he wore a devil costume – so he became known as 'The Devil in Evening Clothes'. After performing a stunning show with two other magicians, 'The Triple Alliance', for four years, he formed the travelling troupe Le Roy, Talma and Bosco – 'Comedians de Mephisto' – and their show travelled the world. He invented many clever illusions and tricks, and even ran a magic company in Hatton Garden, London, selling magical apparatus to his fellow magicians.

His 'Asrah' levitation is still performed today and has been presented by virtually every major illusionist of the past hundred years.

Le Roy was amazingly inventive into old age, long after his regular performing days were over. Then one day he was struck down by a motor car – which was ironic because he'd once invented his own version of car indicators (he called them 'trafficators') before they'd become standard equipment, to try to cut down the number of car accidents. It took him a long time to recover physically, though the accident didn't diminish his spirit – mentally he was just as agile as ever. He filled notebooks with ideas, and invented an appearing elephant trick for one of the largest theatres in New York (although it was never actually performed). He was incredibly secretive about the idea – he didn't even write down the method in his own notebook, so to this day no one is certain how he intended to do it.

And then, years after he had performed his last professional season, he was asked to appear at a convention of magicians to present a single performance at the Heckscher Theatre in New York. Le Roy couldn't resist the temptation and took the show on. But it turned out to be a disaster. Inexperienced assistants tripped out of magic boxes (Le Roy didn't want to tell the assistants how to do the illusions until just before the show in case they told others how they were done), tricks went wrong, rickety apparatus malfunctioned and Le Roy forgot what he was doing. Sadly, in his old age he had lost his former mastery. He didn't even get to the end of the act. He really should never have stepped on to the stage that night.

This demoralised Le Roy much more than the car accident. One day, in a rage of sorrow and disappointment, he took all of the equipment for the Le Roy, Talma and Bosco show that had been stored in his garage for years and flung it on the pavement to be collected by the rubbish men. It was a tragic end to one of the greatest magic shows in history.

I'm lucky enough to have a few of his posters on my wall. The only reason quite a lot of them survived is because Will Goldston, a magic-shop owner who was supposed to be looking after Le Roy's belongings while he was touring the US, used the posters to wrap up books he sold in his shop! So much for taking care of them.

I'd drifted away, thinking about all the stories I'd heard, when a thick Belgium accent rang out behind me in place of Bosco's American twang.

'Ah, so this is ze Hackney house I was hearing about.'

I spun around to find the elegant gentleman I had just been watching onstage standing in my room by the side of the poster frame. Next to him was his wife, Talma. Bosco was nowhere to be seen.

'I am very pleased to meet you,' I said.

Le Roy's face looked kind. He was much smaller than I had expected.

'It is so very interesting to be back here in Hackney,' Le Roy said. One of the ducks seemed particularly friendly towards him, quacking and waddling around his feet. 'Ah, you lovely thing,' he said and picked it up. Talma produced a little box from somewhere. Le Roy placed the quacking duck inside and immediately broke the box into flat pieces – the duck had completely vanished!

'We only have a short time, as we have an evening per-formance and need to reset our show,' Talma said in a surprisingly English accent. 'So let's get straight on with a couple of lessons.'

I was all ears.

'Now,' she said, 'you know my kind of magic – manipulation, sleight of hand – is one of the most difficult to do well . . . It is easy for it to look almost like juggling, because it takes a lot of skill and prestidigitation,' she added.

Prestidigitation – a long word for something that happens fast. It means 'quickness of the fingers'.

Talma continued. 'The point is, you have to practise and practise to make it look not just good – but like magic.'

I remembered one of my favourite TV magicians when I was a kid, a Canadian called Doug Henning. He always used to say, 'You have to practise until the difficult becomes easy, the easy becomes habit and the habit becomes beautiful.' Talma was saying a similar thing.

'If I want to make a coin hidden in my hand seem to come from the air, not just from my hand, I have to act it. I have to imagine the coin is in the air and I have to imagine pulling it out of the air. At the same time I have to do the secret action of bringing it to my fingertips from the hidden position.'

Le Roy was standing by Talma's side. I could see he was very proud of her.

'My finest pupil!' he said, smiling. 'I taught her first, and now I learn from her.'

'Thank you so much, Madame Talma,' I said. 'I will practise to do that, I promise, but some of your skills would take years to learn. Is there something easier you could teach me – something that I can begin with?' I asked cheekily.

Talma looked at me. 'There is no substitute for practice and working hard – and even the simplest things require work. But here is something I can show you.'

✳

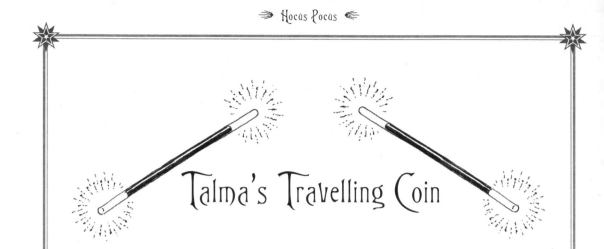

Talma's Travelling Coin

'Do you have four identical coins?' she asked me, sitting down next to the table.

I rummaged around in the little pot on the shelf – I always keep coins in there. I placed four pound coins on the table in front of her. She looked at one curiously. 'A whole pound in a single coin! How extraordinary.'

She took two of the four coins and placed one in each of her upturned palms. She curled her fingers around them, and placed the other two coins carefully on the fingernails of each hand, using her thumb and forefinger.

'Now,' she said, 'I have two coins in each hand – one inside each closed hand, one balanced on top. This is a sort of juggling stunt. The idea is that I have to flick my hand over and catch the two coins balanced on my fingernails in my hands without dropping them.' I watched closely.

'One, two, three,' she said and flicked her hands over. Unfortunately Talma didn't succeed – the two coins that were balanced on her fingernails tumbled on to the table as she flicked her hands over.

'*Mon dieu*,' she said with a smile, 'not enough concentration.' She picked up the two coins that had fallen and placed them back on her upturned closed hands, balancing them on her fingernails.

'I will try again,' she said. 'But I'll concentrate more this time.'

She flicked her hands over quickly. There was a little clinking sound as the coins landed together. 'Aha,' she said, 'I have done it!'

It was a neat move, but to be honest it wasn't much of an illusion. I was surprised that what Talma had shown me seemed to be no more than a demonstration of skill. I looked at her, puzzled.

'That's only a demonstration of skill,' she said, taking the words from my head (I wonder if she was a friend of Alexander). 'That is like juggling. But here is the magic part. This is where I make one of the coins vaporise and travel invisibly from one hand to the other.'

She gestured her closed right hand upwards as if flicking an invisible coin out of it. She followed the path of the invisible coin with her eyes, tracking an imaginary journey over from one hand to the other. As her eyes met her left hand I could swear I heard a coin land inside it.

'So now,' she said, 'one coin has travelled invisibly through space, from my right hand to my left.' She looked at me with a glint in her eye.

'So in this hand I now have only one coin,' she said,

opening up her right hand for me to see. 'And in this hand, I have three.' She opened her left hand, revealing three pound coins which she allowed to fall dramatically on to the table.

Now this was magical! I'd been watching her closely the whole time, and I just couldn't see how she could spirit a coin out of one closed hand into another.

'That was great, Madame,' I said. Then, as cheekily as before, I asked, 'Would you be able to teach it to me?'

Talma smiled. 'There is a secret move, of course, but it happens earlier than you would think. It's when I seemed to make the mistake – when I dropped the two coins off my fingernails. Well, really that was deliberate. The audience will naturally think that the two coins falling on to the table were those balanced on my fingernails.'

'Well, yes,' I said – that was what I thought!

'And that is what you were supposed to think,' said Talma. 'But really, when I flicked my hands over that first time, I opened my left hand a little so that it could catch the coin balanced on my fingernails. At the same time, I opened my right hand just enough to allow the coin inside to fall – just as the coin balanced on my fingernails fell on to the table – and quickly closed my hand again.'

I was beginning to understand this now. So both coins had fallen from the same hand. When she made a point of starting again from the beginning (just after the 'mistake'), she already had two coins in her left hand and absolutely no coins in her right hand. Of course, she pretended to have one coin in each hand, and I had no reason to think differently!

You remember that term 'prestidigitation' – quickness of the fingers? Rarely is it true in magic that fast movements make a trick work – but this is an exception, as Talma explained.

'Keeping my hands closed, I picked up the two coins that had fallen on the table. I put them on the fingernails of each hand and pretended that it was all as before. Of course, I was careful not to open my hands at any point. All I had to do was flick my hands over again. But this time I really did open both hands very slightly to catch each coin balanced on my finger-nails. *Voilà!* I now had one coin in my right hand and three in my left. I then tell the story of the magical journey of the coin and follow the invisible journey with my eyes. I slightly shake my hand when the coin "magically" arrives there – this really completes the illusion of "Talma's Travelling Coin".

'Don't forget that the most important thing – apart from the practice – is the presentation. You have to act the magic, you have to tell the story, otherwise your audience will never join in with their imagination – and that's what really matters.'

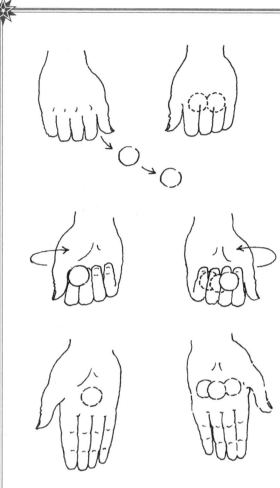

Well, this was just thrilling. It wasn't every day I received a lesson from the Queen of Coins!

Le Roy had been watching Talma with admiration. 'There are many different kinds of magic,' he said. 'This demonstration shows the smallest kind – close-up magic. You cannot do this particular coin trick in a very large theatre! For zat, maybe, you need to perform something bigger – something zat people can see clearly from a long way away. This is why sometimes it is nice to perform a big illusion – making an elephant appear, sawing a lady in half, something like zat.'

He smiled kindly at me. 'So would you like to learn something like this?'

Would I?!

Up, Up and Away!

'Perhaps you would like to levitate someone?' Le Roy asked. 'I will show you a way. It is not a serious thing, but you will have a lot of fun trying it . . . If you will look this way,' Le Roy said, gesturing behind me.

Bosco had reappeared and was standing next to my sofa. He had a large white cloth draped over him, but his head was visible at the top, and his feet, in black shiny shoes, were protruding from the bottom.

'Watch,' said Le Roy, gesturing towards Bosco – and he did indeed seem to start levitating. His head tipped back and I was amazed to see his feet lift off the floor, rising to over a metre in the air. The bottom of the sheet was still touching the ground, unlike the levitation I had seen Le Roy do earlier where Talma had risen at least twice as high. But it was still pretty impressive. Especially considering the size of Bosco!

Well, I'd already tried this as a teenager, practising on my long-suffering grandmother, but I was interested in seeing what Le Roy, the master of levitation, had to say on the subject.

'You can do this one in your living room, and it's nowhere near as elaborate as ze one you saw me do before!' said Le Roy with a smile.

Bosco smiled at me too, before his feet started to descend towards the floor once again and he was vertical. He allowed the cloth to fall away from his shoulders and it gathered in a heap by his feet. He stepped away.

'The secret is very simple.' said Le Roy.

And with that, he rummaged around in the crumpled sheet and removed first one then a second long broom handle. Each handle had a shoe at one end – where you'd expect to see the brush. They were identical to the shoes that Bosco was wearing. I laughed at the funny sight of broom handles with feet.

'So, all your assistant has to do is to hold ze two broom handles under ze sheet. If you are going to ask your grandmother, make sure she is supple enough and tell 'er not to strain too much! Make sure her shoes are poking out from under ze bottom of ze cloth. And then, slowly, get her to tilt

her head back
and at ze same
time swing ze
broom handles
with ze shoes
attached slowly
upwards, keeping
them both parallel
and together as if
they are her own
feet rising off ze
ground. Use a
big sheet from a
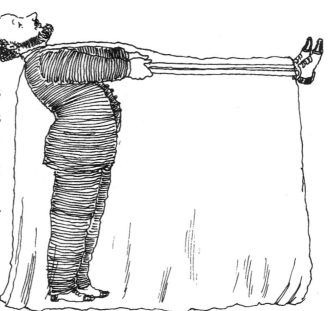
double bed to cover her, to make sure zat ze sheet is always
touching ze ground. Otherwise, the audience will see her real
feet standing on ze floor! Ze success is all in ze acting.'

Le Roy and Talma stood there together. 'Of course, this is
not like my "Asrah" mystery,' he said. 'It's more of a fun thing
to try – not a great mystery. But zen you will have to study
magic for many years before you can perform a great levitation
act! Oh – and you will need to appear in a theatre too.'

Although I longed for the day that I could stand on a stage
and perform a grand levitation illusion like his amazing
'Asrah', I was grateful to be shown any kind of levitation by
Servais Le Roy, one of the greatest magicians who ever lived.

Just at that point, Bosco came running back into the room,
holding a large chicken and balancing an egg on his nose. 'It's

time to prepare,' he announced.

'So now we have to get ready for our performance,' said Talma, picking up the remaining duck in one hand and a corner of the white sheet in the other. 'It has been very good to meet you.'

And with that she and Le Roy lifted the sheet, Bosco standing between them, until they were out of sight. With a little flicking motion they threw it up in the air and when the sheet fell to the ground they had vanished in the blink of an eye. The only thing that remained was a single white feather, fluttering slowly to the ground in front of me.

Chapter 5

Soirées Fantastiques

WHAT A TRIPLE WHAMMY! Le Roy, Talma and Bosco — invention, precision and laughs. Every time I saw the trio on their poster, I had to smile. And I took everything Le Roy and Talma said to heart. Practice, practice, practice!

So what with rehearsing my routines and just about keeping up with my workload, I'd been so busy that I'd forgotten all about my garden. One morning I looked out of the back window and got a bit of a shock. The grass was at least a foot high (I couldn't even see the path), and fallen leaves were scattered all over it. The bushes and other plants looked a bit sorry for themselves, and a lot of crisp packets and plastic bags were scattered about. There's a wall around the garden, but the wind blows all sorts of stuff in from the market down the road.

After seeing how sorry it looked, I set to work. I cleared the rubbish and put it in the bin, and swept up the leaves into a tidy heap. I thought I'd try to perk up the plants by giving them some water and a feed.

I was standing on the path, happily tip-ping the watering can over a bush, when I heard an odd noise. *Click-clack, tok-tik, click-clack* — where was it coming from?

I put down the can and looked around the garden but couldn't

see anything, so I just shrugged and started watering again. *Could be a bird*, I thought — *one of those clever mimics that have started copying all sorts of noises*. I'd found out from a TV show that starlings can imitate the trilling of a mobile phone. That must get a lot of people in the street fumbling in their bags and pockets.

On the other hand, the longer the mysterious sound went on, the more I suspected that another wizardly apparition might be along any minute — and I wasn't prepared to be ambushed by a magician in the open air. Much as I wanted to see my magical visitors, I'd rather they kept inside the house. I didn't want any more skinny sorcerers leaping about the back garden with lions and horses – it'd upset the neighbours.

Whatever, I wasn't going to be caught unawares, so I crouched down by the side of a somewhat overgrown laurel bush, trying as best as I could to disguise myself in the branches, and waited.

And waited, and waited. I was there for ages and the only thing that seemed to be appearing was backache (it's tough work trying to look like a plant). No sign of any master magicians, so I got up again, feeling a bit daft. Even next-door's cat was looking down at me from the wall as if I was barmy. Well, she seemed to be quite bothered about something, so I stood up and pretended I'd been weeding. The cat didn't seem at all impressed and walked along the wall, looking very snooty.

The strange thing was, I realised I could still hear the click-clacking sound – in fact it seemed to be getting nearer and nearer. So I decided to go inside the house and keep a lookout from there in case anything strange happened.

As I walked towards the open back door I looked into the far wall of the room and noticed an odd thing. One of my favourite posters was looking decidedly – well, blank. The gold frame was looking as splendid as ever but all that remained of the image itself was the curly border around the outside with the lettering underneath: *Robert-Houdin Soirées Fantastiques* (that means 'fantastic evenings'!). There was no sign at all of the famous French magician or his equally famous mechanical friend, Antonio Diavolo, who were normally depicted. I stood there for a moment, puzzled, gazing through the door, trying to work out what this meant, when – *whoosh*! A gust of wind caught the door and – *BANG!* – slammed it shut. I'd have to get back in with my key.

I reached into my pocket, expecting to find it straightaway but instead found a crumpled old receipt that had been through the wash a few times – there was no sign of my key. There was, however, a hole in the pocket, which explained things. *Oh no!* I thought. *It could be anywhere!* With grass that long, I'd have a job finding something as big as a back door, let alone a key.

Meanwhile, I could hear that strange noise again. It was like the sound of an old grandfather clock being wound up, in fits and starts. I looked suspiciously around the lawn – but there was nothing to be seen except my wilting plants (and a few crisp packets I'd missed).

And then I noticed something very odd. I looked over to the bush I'd been hiding under – and several large blooms had appeared. I could swear they looked like they were still growing! I was pretty certain there wasn't so much as a bud there a few minutes ago – my fertiliser might have been called 'Miracle Plant Feed' but this was ridiculous!

Hmmm . . . and as I was staring at the blossoms, which were beautiful (but didn't look like any flowers I'd seen before – they seemed more like feathers), another weird noise started. This time it sounded very near.

I walked across the grass, looking carefully at the plants, seeing if any others were showing accelerated signs of life (I usually succeed in killing plants, not making them grow, so I was feeling quite pleased with myself!), when – *BOSH!* – something swung into my face. Startled, I stepped back and looked up. No wonder the cat was looking puzzled. Right in front of my eyes was one of the most astonishing things I'd ever seen!

A little wooden figure, no bigger than a doll, was perched on a small branch right in front of me. He was dressed very smartly in a burgundy jacket, green satin trousers, a shiny red waistcoat, a bright blue bow tie and a bright red beret. He was looking at me with a very cheeky expression on his face, swinging his legs to and fro and making the branch move. It was the movement of his legs that was making the funny mechanical clicking sound.

I stared at him, unable to say anything, but I knew exactly who he was. Antonio Diavolo, the amazing acrobatic doll, was one of Mr Robert-Houdin's most famous creations.

'Are you Antonio?' I finally asked the little man cautiously. He nodded his head, and then his little hands swung down to his sides, apparently gripping the branch.

'Careful!' I said – but the little man was determined. He flicked his knees forward and before I knew it he was swinging back and forth on the branch with his arms, making the click-clacking sound. I watched in amazement as he lifted himself back on to his perch.

And then – quite suddenly – he dropped back. I gasped, thinking he would fall, and then realised he was just performing another stunt. He was now swinging upside down on the branch, with only his bent knees holding him on. Then, within moments, Antonio was swinging spectacularly from the branch with his miniature hands.

'And now, little one, you must let go,' said a deep voice in a thick French accent that seemed to come from nowhere, and before I knew it the wooden child was flying towards me. I'm normally rubbish at catching things like tennis balls but by instinct I caught little Antonio as he flew through the air, his wooden limbs flopping into my hands.

Phew, I thought, and before I had caught my breath the deep voice spoke again, echoing around the garden.

'Monsieur – may I introduce myself?'

From behind the bush stepped a handsome man – tall and slim, and wearing immaculate evening clothes. He was unmistakable.

The father of modern magic himself: Jean Eugène Robert-Houdin.

Before I had a chance to shut my mouth, which had fallen open in surprise, he spoke again, with great politeness. 'May I borrow an 'andkerchief from you, Monsieur?'

I happened to have one in my pocket (the one without the hole) – an old one given to me by a great-aunt (who insists on embroidering initials on everything and gives me handkerchiefs *every* birthday).

Cradling the little doll with one arm, I took the hanky out of my pocket with the other hand and passed it to the Frenchman. '*Merci,*' he said. 'Now, watch closely.' And he rolled the handkerchief into a ball between his hands. I noticed that his fingers were long and slender – like a pianist's. Next, he took a magic wand from his pocket and tapped his hand. He uncurled his fingers one by one with a flourish. My handkerchief had vanished.

'If you please, Monsieur,' he said, and gestured to the other side of the garden with his magic wand.

Houdin was gesturing towards the bush that had started to bloom a few minutes before. As I watched, the flowers grew even bigger and then full-size oranges began to appear on its branches. Robert-Houdin walked over to the little tree and plucked the oranges off it – throwing them across the lawn to me (trying to hold on to Antonio, I rather clumsily dropped two of them). Only one orange remained, and as I stared, it divided slowly into four pieces, peeling back to reveal what looked like a piece of cloth inside, with two corners poking up. Just then, two red and green mechanical butterflies fluttered out of the bush, and each settled on a corner of the cloth. Beating their colourful wings, they both flew up, pulling out the piece of material – they had to be the strongest butterflies I'd ever seen!

The cloth looked familiar – hang on a minute, that was my handkerchief! I absolutely knew because it had 'PK' embroidered on it! And the most surprising thing was that in the centre, tied on with a little bow, was my back-door key! Now – how on earth did that happen?

The butterflies dropped their burden into the magician's outstretched hand and disappeared behind the bush. He untied the key and gave it back to me, along with the hanky.

'If you will open your back door, Monsieur, I will prepare the rest of my show,' he said.

I opened the door and he strolled calmly in, murmuring, 'Kindly give me a few minutes, Monsieur. Antonio will let you know when I am ready.'

I stood outside in the yard looking down at the little wooden figure, as the elegant Frenchman disappeared into the back room.

Mechanical Marvels

No, I haven't been spelling his name wrong – it's not the famous Houdini-with-an-i. Houdini himself was originally called Erich Weisz (not a name to inspire wonder, with all due respect) – he admired Robert-Houdin so much that he changed his name to sound like him. (By the way, being French, Robert-Houdin would have pronounced his name as Roe-bare-Oo-dan.)

He used to be called just Jean Eugène Robert – he got the hyphen when he married his wife, Josèphe Houdin. He decided to take the double-barrelled version when he went into business, and kept it as a stage name – at least for a while. It was a bit of a mouthful, and, except on posters, people usually referred to him as plain Houdin, so I'll do the same from now on.

He took his time actually getting on stage – he was nearly forty when he gave his first public performance. He was born in 1805, in the French town of Blois, the son of a watchmaker, destined to follow in his father's footsteps.

It was a sheer accident that set him on his magical career. The story goes that when he was working as an apprentice watchmaker, learning the ropes (or rather gears, cogs and all the other bits of machinery), he went to buy a book on horology (as the study of clocks and watches is known). The bookseller was busy and gave him the wrong book by mistake – a wrong book that turned out to be very much the right book for Jean. It was an encyclopedia of 'scientific amusements' – the secrets behind simple scientific experiments and conjuring tricks.

Young Jean was fascinated and began to learn all he could about magic, taking lessons in sleight of hand and practising as much as he could. He was already very good with his hands – he would have to be, making all the intricate working parts of clocks and watches. In fact, as a child, he had made his own clockwork toys – they really worked. When he was older he built amazing 'mystery clocks'. These were ornate clocks with completely transparent glass faces supported on transparent stems. The hands seemed to turn without any mechanism.

Not that Houdin originally planned to become a full-time magician – he was happy being an amateur, entertaining his friends and family with his skills. He came to the attention of a wealthy neighbour, a count, who introduced him into high society. Eventually Houdin did turn professional, giving his first public performance in July 1845. He was so nervous that the show was a disaster, but he wasn't put off. He continued to practise until he became highly skilled. Soon he was a huge hit, and went on to become one of the most inventive and influential magicians who has ever lived.

His shows, which included mind-reading and ingenious mechanical toys (or 'automata'), were a great hit with audiences. He invented a levitation called 'The Ethereal Suspension'. Around this time a chemical called ether was being introduced into medicine, which made people go to sleep during operations. (Before then people had to stay awake while they were undergoing surgery – not much fun.) The public had heard about this new discovery, and it seemed very mysterious and powerful. So Houdin claimed that ether could make his son, Emile, lighter than air, and demonstrated this by suspending him horizontally in space with only the tip of his elbow resting on a balanced walking stick.

Houdin was a master at using science to baffle his audiences – of course, 'The Ethereal Suspension' did not rely on ether as its method, but Houdin had his hidden assistants pour the potent chemical on to a hot iron so that the audience would smell it! The audience was convinced that they had been shown a clever scientific demonstration. Houdin often really did use science – but more often than not as a hidden secret behind some of his most amazing illusions. And he didn't just limit his science to his shows – he was one of the first people in the world to use an electric light bulb. His home in Blois, near Paris, was filled with amazing mechanical creations, such as a burglar alarm and automatic gates. Not bad for the 1850s!

His other great contribution to magic was his costume. It may seem obvious now for a magician to be dressed in smart evening clothes, but before Houdin magicians were more likely to be dressed in cloaks and pointy hats. At the time he was considered highly fashionable, dressed in an immaculate tail coat and a bow tie. Even today people dress like Houdin to perform magic (though now it's not so fashionable or original – I think a lot of them would do better in cloaks and pointy hats!). Houdin took magic from a low art form to a highly respected place in French society.

In the early 1850s Houdin performed abroad, and then began to think of retiring. But something happened in 1856 which makes him unique among stage magicians. He helped to stop a rebellion – in real life. It's just like those stories in old children's books.

It was in the days when France had an empire and ruled other lands apart from France. There'd been a revolt in the French-controlled African state of Algiers, when a religious group called the Marabouts went about encouraging tribal leaders to become independent. They were known as wonder-workers – that is, illusionists – and the French government thought that perhaps one of their own wonder-workers might be able to impress them; to persuade them that the French were greater magicians!

So Houdin performed several times in Algiers, with all the leaders in the audience. Among other acts, he produced cannonballs from an empty hat and made silver coins flow into a closed crystal chest – sending the message that France was strong and could go where it wanted. His crowning piece of propaganda was to deprive a man of his strength!

Houdin placed a wooden cash box on the floor, and invited a volunteer, an Arab, to lift it. No problem. Then the magician asked him to lift it again. This time, no chance.

The man strained and strained – but couldn't lift it an inch. Suddenly, he yelled and fell over in pain, then ran off the stage, terrified.

Of course the box was secretly prepared: it had a hidden iron bottom, and Houdin had fixed a strong electromagnet under the carpet (another clever use of science). When this was switched on, the strongest man in the world couldn't have lifted it. (The volunteer yelled, by the way, when an electric shock was sent through the metal handles of the box. Charming.)

For his next magical demonstration, Houdin made a young

Arab boy disappear. One minute he was standing on a table and covered with a large cloth, and the next – he'd vanished. Panic! Everyone in the audience stampeded out of the theatre.

Today these feats would still look impressive, but audiences would recognise them as clever demonstrations of illusion. In those days many people were very superstitious. Houdin's conjuring skills would have seemed supernatural to them. And remember – this was long before most people ever imagined that the power of electricity could be harnessed.

The rebels were highly impressed and promised to behave. (The same tactic wouldn't work now!) Mission accomplished, Houdin returned to his grateful country, where he gave one final performance, then retired to write books and conduct scientific experiments.

Just like his books, many of his automata and mystery clocks have survived to entertain people now.

Talking of which, I felt the little doll twitch in my hands and looked down. His tiny head was nodding back and forth and his legs were dangling off the side of my hand and kicking vigorously. *Ah, Houdin must be ready for his show.*

✦

As I walked in I couldn't believe what I saw. All of my furniture had disappeared and in its place were fancy tables with curvy legs, decorated with vases, flowers and elaborate little dishes. I put Antonio on a table right next to the window, where he sat still, looking quite unacrobatic.

Houdin himself was standing beside one of the tables. 'You 'ave already seen two of my greatest specialities,' he announced. 'Permit me to show you some more.

'I would like to demonstrate my most favourite subject – zat of prestidigitation!' he said with an elegant flourish of his hand.

There's that word again. Talma had been keen on that too. Pres-ti-di-git-ta-tion – sleight of hand. Literally, quickness of the fingers. (By the way, I looked up the French for magician, or conjuror – know what it is? *Le prestidigitateur*. Very impressive. I think I'll call myself that.)

Houdin was talking to me again. 'Ze art of conjuring, my

friend, depends on practising 'ard with ze fingers and keeping ze mind agile. To become a truly great magician, it is necessary to 'ave a good general knowledge of science, and to be able to apply a few of its principles.' As he spoke he repeatedly fanned a pack of cards in front of him in a variety of patterns, and started shuffling them using only one hand.

'But ze most vital requirement is greatness of manipulation – dexterity – combined with special mental alertness. It is possible to play ze conjuror without these things by using clever apparatus. But zis is not clever – it is of ze same order as zat of ze musician who produces a tune by turning ze 'andle of a barrel organ!'

Right, I thought. *Got that.* I would write everything down in my notebook when I got a moment. Everything he said must be true – he's not known as the 'father of modern magic' for nothing.

'In ozzer words, you should not be LAZY with your PRACTICE,' he said abruptly. I felt like telling him that actually I had been practising a lot recently – but I bet that wouldn't have impressed him.

Houdin clapped his hands together and the playing cards seemed to vanish before my eyes. He had finished his lecture, and was now lifting up what looked like two big flat pieces of black cardboard. They were held together with a wide piece of ribbon as a hinge. 'I would like to show you now my portfolio,' he said.

My eyes widened. Portfolios are what artists keep their

pictures in – I never knew he was a painter. I hoped he would show me some pictures of his mystery clocks.

Houdin placed the portfolio on to two little trestles.

'Ze most simple of ze laws of nature is zat ze container must be larger than ze contents,' he announced. 'But 'ere it is ze opposite – this demonstrates ze impossible becoming possible!'

He then shouted 'Voilà!' and pulled out – oh, just two drawings of Paris in the 1850s. Very pretty, but they could have been in the portfolio all along.

'Of course,' Houdin went on, 'in Paris ze ladies are very beautiful, and they like to wear lovely things.' With that, he pulled out two large elaborate hats, decorated with ribbons and fresh flowers. I laughed and applauded – now that was a bit more impressive.

'Of course,' he said again, 'it is good to cover your 'ead in case something should fly above you.' With a twinkle in his eye, Houdin pulled out three beautiful doves, which flapped their wings – they were real enough! He placed them on a small perch at the side.

'And now it is time for ze dinner,' he said, pulling out three huge brass pots one after the other in quick succession – one filled with beans, one with flames leaping out and another filled with boiling water. As if that wasn't enough he reached again inside the portfolio – which had after all started completely flat – and pulled out the most enormous bird cage with little birds hopping about inside!

I applauded wildly, as Houdin folded the portfolio completely flat again. He made a little bow, but he looked as if he had not entirely finished.

'I would like you to meet my son, Emile,' he said, and tapped the top of the portfolio with his magic wand three times. The top swung back and, impossibly, a little boy of about seven years old popped out, smiling . . . He and his father bowed while I clapped like mad – this really was fantastic. Fantastic! And right in front of my eyes. No wonder he frightened those rebels. If I didn't know better, I'd think he had supernatural powers too. (And how handy, I thought, a child who fits into a portfolio – I'd have to try that with my niece and nephew.)

The Invisible Card

When I finally stopped applauding, Houdin stepped forward. 'You are too kind,' he said. 'Allow me to share with you one of my ozzer most favourite pieces of magic. Do you 'ave a pack of cards?'

Of course, that was like asking Lafayette if he had any dog nibbles.

I rummaged around in a drawer, the same one that Alexander had found my highlighter pen in a few months before, and produced a lovely pack that I only used on special occasions. Houdin took them from me and looked at the cards admiringly as he shuffled them neatly in his hands.

'Now, I will ask you, please, to take one card – any card you like – from ze pack.'

Houdin fanned the cards towards me with an elegant swish. They appeared to be perfectly spaced. I picked a card – it was the Three of Hearts.

'Now, do not show it to me,' he said. 'Remember what it is, and place it back somewhere in ze pack.'

I pushed my card into the centre of the pack, making sure it went all the way in and was level with the rest of the cards.

Houdin squared the cards up in his hands.

'Now, this piece of magic is very impressive,' he said. 'I will perform two magic effects in one. I 'ave lost your card in ze pack – I cannot know where it is. I will now pull it out of ze pack, but at the same time it will become – invisible!'

I watched closely. Houdin seemed to be concentrating as his hand ran down the side of the cards.

'AHA – I 'ave it!' he exclaimed, and he whisked his right hand forward. His left hand was still holding the cards.

'Is zat your card?' he said.

I looked at the hand he was holding up – but it was empty!

'I can't see a card,' I said, wondering what he was getting at.

'Zat is because – it is invisible!' he exclaimed with a twinkle in his eye.

I clearly didn't look too sure.

'I can tell you, Monsieur, zat this is your card. I am 'olding it – but you are not at all convinced? So, let me now turn your invisible card over, so zat it will be ze only one face up in ze pack. See – I push it back into ze pack.'

As Houdin spoke, he acted as if he was flipping over the invisible card and pushing it back into the pack.

'Now, I will click my fingers, and your card will become visible again!' he said with a smile. 'So now, if it was your card zat I invisibly took from ze pack, it should be ze only one which is turned over.'

I nodded in agreement, and Houdin fanned the cards out slowly. I watched the backs of the cards carefully. About halfway through I saw a flash of white – one card had indeed turned over. Houdin spread the pack out further and I could see it was the Three of Hearts, my chosen card!

'That's amazing,' I exclaimed.

Houdin smiled at me. 'Well, Monsieur,' he said, 'this is indeed an interesting piece of magic. You know I said zat you 'ad to learn sleight of hand? Well, this is a good starter sleight-of-hand trick – it really is quite easy. The success is all in ze acting.'

'The acting?' I asked.

'Your presentation – ze thing that makes ze magic – it is

acting. A magician is really an actor playing ze part of a magician – you 'ave to act ze magic. All talk of turning ze card invisible, it is a story for ze audience to make them interested in what you are doing. It is like a little theatre play – you give them ze story and ze magic happens inside ze story.'

I thought I understood, but I was a little distracted as I caught sight of the neighbour's cat sitting on the windowsill outside. He seemed to be staring intently at Antonio Diavolo lying on the table. It wouldn't have taken Alexander: The Man Who Knows to tell what the cat was thinking – it was licking its lips . . .

I shook myself and turned back to Houdin. 'I would love you to show me the secret, so that I might be able to perform it, Monsieur Houdin.'

'This requires very simple preparation,' said the magician. 'It takes only one second. You 'ave to turn over ze very bottom card in ze pack – just one card, ze only card facing up. That is 'ow you start ze trick. When you lent me ze cards I did zat when you were distracted. Then you spread ze cards out in your 'ands face down, making sure you do not show ze card which is turned over at ze bottom. Ask ze spectator to take one card out but not to look at it yet. Once they 'ave taken it out, square ze cards up in your 'ands. Now is ze second secret move. You say to ze spectator, "Please look at your card now." As they lift the card up to look at it you simply turn ze pack of cards over in your hand. Now it is upside down, but because you turned over one card on ze bottom of ze pack, it looks exactly ze same as before.'

I was beginning to see!

Houdin continued. 'You must keep the cards squared up – if they spread out, the audience would see that ze pack is really face up with only one card face down on ze top. Ask ze spectator to push their card into ze centre. Once they have done this, take ze pack and square it up in your hands. Really, ze trick is almost done – but now you 'ave to tell ze story about turning ze card invisible. This is ze part of ze most importance – ze acting!

'So now you tell ze spectator ze little story, that you will pull their card from ze pack and it will also turn invisible. You take a moment and pretend to locate ze card, and then two things 'appen at once. You act as if you are pulling ze card from ze pack with your left 'and. Really you do nothing with this hand except lift it up in ze air empty. Say, "Is this your card?" At ze same moment, when your spectator is distracted by looking at your empty 'and, you turn ze cards over again with your right 'and so zat they are once again face down. Ze timing of this is very important – you want ze audience to be looking away from your secret move. This is what magician's call "misdirection" – drawing ze audience's eyes away from ze secret. It is one of ze most important parts of magic technique.'

Things were getting even clearer.

'Now ze trick is done. All you 'ave to do is spread ze cards out in your 'ands once again. You will find zat in ze middle of the pack is ze spectator's card turned face up among all ze cards zat are face down. Make sure you do not spread out ze bottom two cards otherwise ze audience will see ze reversed card at ze bottom of ze pack.'

I was impressed. It didn't sound too difficult for such a mystifying effect.

'Remember,' Houdin urged one more time, 'you 'ave to act ze story – and make it fun for ze spectator.'

Emile, who had been quietly sitting on the floor, playing with a wooden mechanical toy, had now got up. He was holding Antonio in his hands. 'Look at Antonio, Papa,' he said. The puppet was twitching.

'Ah oui,' said Houdin, "e wants to go 'ome.'

Houdin handed me back the cards and headed out of the back door into the garden. As we all walked out, the sun was shining on the little bush. The flowers were shrinking away.

Houdin held out his hand. 'Monsieur, it was a pleasure to meet you,' he said, bowing slightly.

I shook his hand enthusiastically, saying, 'It was a pleasure and an honour to meet *you*, Monsieur.'

Houdin smiled and produced a magic wand out of his pocket, pointing it up in the air. There was a bang and a small flame flew out of the end of the wand and shot up high in the air. As I followed it with my eyes, the flame somehow transformed into a little silk streamer which fluttered down towards me with a shower of confetti. I caught it and opened it out. On it was written the words: *Au revoir.* When I looked up, Houdin, Emile and Antonio had vanished without a trace.

Misdirection! I thought to myself, smiling, as I stepped towards my Poster Room – which now looked entirely back to normal.

Chapter 6

All Done by Kindness

MAGIC WAS COMING OUT OF my ears! Well, that's what it felt like. On top of Alexander's mystical mind-reading, Lafayette's spectacular 'Lion's Bride' illusion, and Le Roy with Talma and Bosco, I'd been knocked sideways by the impeccable prestidigitations of Robert-Houdin, not to mention the magical acrobatic skills of little Antonio Diavolo.

Right from the start of the magical manifestations, I'd kept a little notebook so I'd remember as much as possible. I laughed at myself now – it looked like I'd need a much bigger book! I was learning so much from these old masters. It would probably take me several lifetimes to learn everything they knew. Meanwhile, I'd taken on board one of the most important lessons: I'd have to practise and practise each

illusion – and practise again – to make it convincing to an audience.

And anyway, it was such a good excuse not to do any more house jobs than were absolutely necessary. I'd been meaning to buy a new vacuum cleaner – my current one seemed to be leaving more dirt on the floor than it picked up, on the rare occasions I used it. And I'd never got around to fixing the broken cupboard door in my kitchen – so difficult to fit domestic chores in between visits from master magicians and all that rehearsing!

In fact the house had been quiet for a few weeks and I'd been practising quite a bit for a great job that had come in. I had received a letter in a very grand-looking envelope from the Around Eightieth Agency asking me to appear in a variety show in a big London theatre in the spring of next year. The letter said they had been following my career, and although the date was not fixed it was a definite booking and I should prepare for it. It was signed at the bottom in bold black ink, but I couldn't make out the name. I'd not heard of the company, but then these theatrical companies often choose unusual names, and I was thrilled to be asked. Perhaps my magical teachers and practising were beginning to come up trumps. The show wasn't for a while but I was very excited about it; I had even decided to save up and buy a new suit for the occasion.

But I couldn't practise all the time and one morning, lying half asleep, I decided I really would catch up on some of those boring chores. I rolled out of bed and threw some clothes on, and was stumbling down the stairs a bit bleary-eyed when I noticed something odd. The door to the Poster Room was firmly shut, and I was certain I'd left it open the night before. And there was something else: dangling from a nail that had been hammered into the back of the door was a little white card. *That wasn't there last night*, I thought to myself. It had some words printed on it in very small type. I walked down the last couple of steps so that I could read them:

£1,000 reward offered to anyone – man, woman or child – who does not find these doors open at 9 a.m.

Hmmm, I thought. *It looks like today won't be quite as I was expecting.* I tried the handle but the door was firmly shut. I could hear the sound of someone inside tinkling away at the piano as if they were tuning it. I clearly had visitors. No chance of housework, then. What a shame.

I looked at my watch – it was ten to nine, plenty of time for a cuppa before whatever was in store. I went into the kitchen and filled the kettle with water, and watched while it came to the boil, staring into the steam drifting out of the spout, wondering what adventures were to come. I dropped a teabag into my favourite mug and tipped the kettle over it, expecting to see a steady stream of boiling water. Well, you would, wouldn't you?

By now I should have learned to expect the unexpected . . .

What came out of the kettle was orange! And stone cold! What? I poured out a little more into the sink. It smelt sweet – yes, it was orange juice!

I slammed down the kettle and grabbed another mug from the cupboard – was this a dream? I tipped the kettle slowly.

What came out this time was a rich dark brown with little wisps of steam coming off it. I cautiously sniffed it. Hmm, hot chocolate. Smelt good, but it was tea that I wanted . . .

Shaking my head at the absurdity, I took some more mugs out of the cupboard and lined them up on the kitchen table, tipping the kettle over them one by one. First there was blackcurrant juice, then milk, then lemonade, followed by something fizzy (I think it was cola), something yellow and a bit lumpy (banana milkshake), then steaming hot coffee and some other things that I didn't recognise. By now I was laughing with delight – I must have had a dozen cups and mugs lined up, all of them filled with different things! Very strange: apart from the fact that it was producing an amazing variety of drinks, my little kettle normally only manages to fill about four mugs.

But still no tea! So I pulled out some more mugs and cups and carried on (something cold and green filled one – I didn't like the look of that). Finally the last cup was filled – hot tea at last! I picked it up, leaving the others on the table, and looked at my watch. It was just coming up to nine – time to see what adventures awaited me . . .

I headed back to the locked door. It was still firmly shut with the little sign on it. I stood there watching the second hand of my watch approach the hour. I had an excited feeling about who I might be going to see – the magical kettle which poured 'any drink called for' was a very famous illusion of a truly great British magician. I wondered briefly what would happen if the door didn't open. Would I be £1,000 richer? I hoped not. I'd happily *pay* £1,000 to see this man perform – if it turned out to be who I hoped it would be.

But, sure enough, at nine o'clock on the dot I heard a click as the door was unlocked from the inside, and it swung open.

An immaculately dressed gentleman was standing just inside the room, a neat moustache nesting under his nose, along with a very impressive beard on his chin. He was obviously the usher.

'Tickets, please, ladies and gentlemen,' he said in a well-spoken English accent, which seemed odd because I was the only person waiting to come in.

Then he caught sight of me.

'Ah – welcome, sir. Please take your seat.' He indicated a

wooden chair that I didn't recognise from anywhere. In fact there wasn't much in my room I recognised at all, apart from my big table pushed against one wall. Now there were rows of wooden chairs with Egyptian carvings on them, leading up to a little stage hung with deep red curtains. The seat the man had pointed to was carved from very dark wood, and on the arms were the faces of Egyptian cats. On the chair was a programme with the headline:

Maskelyne and Devant presents
David Devant
All done by kindness!

A feeling of tremendous excitement rushed through me – I was right about who it was going to be!

I opened the programme and scanned it quickly.

Mr David Devant will present a selection from his repertoire of Original Mysteries and Magical Problems, including 'The Artist's Dream'. An artist is working on a painting of the woman he loves – sadly, she has recently died. Overtired, he falls asleep and dreams that the charming picture comes to life.

There were a couple of other things listed too: *'The Magic Mirror – Glimpses of the Past, Present and Future'* and *'After a short interlude – Biff or the D. D. Rays'*. I was intrigued and very excited. A personal performance from one of the greatest magicians of all time!

The lights faded in the room and the curtains swept open. Sure enough, just as the programme had promised, the stage setting was an artist's studio. A man was standing by an easel, working on a picture of a very beautiful woman. *This must be the lady he loves – probably his wife*, I thought, *the one who's just died.* The artist was played by Devant himself (I recognised him from my poster), dressed in a smock and beret. He suddenly seemed to become weary, covered the painting with a small curtain, and fell asleep slumped over his paintbrushes. After a few moments a strange figure appeared to one side – obviously a woman, but wearing a costume that made her look like a giant butterfly. She spent some time fluttering her wings mysteriously and walking around from one side of the stage to the other (getting into a flap, you might say!). Then she went up to the painting and gently waved her wings towards it. What was she doing?

Obviously working some kind of magic spell, I thought to myself. As she stood there in front of the easel, the little curtain swept to one side to reveal the beautiful lady from the painting in flesh and blood! The canvas itself was now completely blank – the painting had come to life. Now, of course, this was something I had seen in my posters, but Devant had done this throughout his career in front of hundreds of audiences live on stage!

The elegant lady then stepped forward and approached her sleeping husband. She spookily went up to him and started to stroke his arm. *That'll be a surprise for him,* I thought, *waking up to see the ghost of the lady he loves.* She stayed there for a few moments, and although the artist was stirring he didn't wake up. *Too bad,* I thought, *she's come back all the way from the other world and he sleeps through it. At least when my posters come alive I pay them attention.* Then I remembered – the programme had said this was all happening in his dream.

The deceased wife had stopped stroking her husband's arm and stepped back up towards the painting – it seemed like she had run out of time – and the little curtain in front of the canvas dropped completely in front of her. By this time the moth-like lady was flapping her wings even more. Then, with a jolt, the artist suddenly awoke. He'd missed his wife by a split second! He ran to the curtain and tore it back – as if he knew his wife would be behind it. But all that remained was the painted picture on the easel – the lady had turned back into her portrait. The artist then grabbed the picture off the easel, turning it around, looking like he was in a desperate rage – the flesh and blood lady had definitely disappeared!

Then the artist noticed the strange figure next to him – he looked startled (wouldn't you if a giant moth was fluttering around you? I find them unnerving enough when they're normal sized!). 'Spirit of Mercy, what does this mean?' he shouted (ah – so that was who she was supposed to be). What happened next was amazing. The lady raised the butterfly wings in front of her face, and Devant approached –

but the moment he went to grab her she just vanished into thin air! Not with a puff of smoke or anything – just like she had caved in on herself and dissolved. Stunning! The artist cried out and then clutched his heart – collapsing to the stage in a very theatrical pose. I think he was meant to have died of shock. The curtain closed and the music played a melancholy final chord.

Well, I thought, applauding like mad and still amazed at what I had just seen, *they did like a bit of drama in the old days!* Or melodrama, more like.

So there I was, astonished by Devant's short magic play. I remembered what Houdin had said about a magician really being an actor playing the part of a magician – this seemed to be proof in front of my eyes! The illusions I'd just seen – 'The Artist's Dream' and 'The Mascot Moth' – were two of Devant's most famous, though he didn't always combine them like this. 'The Mascot Moth' disappearing lady was the illusion he considered to be his finest achievement – it was referred to as Devant's 'Trickiest Trick'! He'd dreamed it up one night by imagining a human moth flying into a candle flame . . .

I couldn't wait for the next bit of the show.

Devant then came through the curtain, dressed in a smart suit, smiling broadly.

'I welcome you to the show this morning,' he said in a charming voice. 'As you watch the things you see before your eyes, you may indeed wonder – how is that done? Well, ladies and gentlemen,' he went on, with a twinkle in his eye, 'I take great pleasure in telling you. I would like to assure you that it is all done – by kindness!' And he gave a small bow.

'Next,' he announced, 'I would like to ask someone from the audience to come up to assist – perhaps you?' He didn't have too great a choice – there were only two of us. Fortunately he pointed to the usher, and he walked up on to the stage.

The curtains opened to reveal a large mirror on a wheeled stand in the centre – it was quite a bit taller than Devant and as wide as the front of a car. Now that was a big mirror! Devant spun the mirror around so that I could see all sides – nothing there, it just looked like an ordinary mirror. 'Please, sir,' said Devant, 'would you stand in front of the mirror. I would like you to stare at your own face. Look at it carefully. Do you know what you can see? This is your present.'

I looked at the man's reflection. He seemed strangely familiar to me.

'Now,' Devant continued, 'I would like to take you back to your past.'

He waved his hand around the mirror. Slowly and eerily the man's face in the reflection seemed to melt away. For a few moments nothing happened and then a tiny red glow appeared in the centre of the glass. The glow seemed to expand more and more and suddenly a terrifying face appeared – a nasty-looking bright red imp! I don't know about anyone else, but it gave me an awful shock! It made the imps on Kellar's poster look positively friendly.

'That is your frightening past,' Devant intoned, adding, with a glint in his eye, 'You were often thought of as a little devil!'

As the man was staring into the mirror, the magician announced, 'You have seen your present and your past. Now let me take you to your future.'

With this, Devant waved his hand over the front of the glass. The scary figure of the imp dissolved into nothing – just as something else started to appear, something white and hazy. In a couple of moments this had turned into a pretty girl dressed in an old-fashioned-looking wedding dress.

The man went to touch her, but – 'NO!' said Devant. 'Not yet. That is your future.'

The next thing happened very quickly. As the bride faded away, Devant picked up a large cloak. He swirled around and within what seemed like a split second the cloak fell to the floor. Devant had vanished in front of our eyes! The man standing on the stage looked very bewildered. A moment later another light started to appear in the mirror. As it grew in intensity I could see exactly what it was — an image of Devant himself. And eerily it spoke: 'I thank you for your assistance, sir, and ask you to return to your seat.'

I applauded loudly as the man walked to the back of the rows of seats. The curtains closed in front of Devant's face, mysteriously looming in the mirror.

I was truly amazed by this demonstration — but was hoping for still more. As I sat there in anticipation, I glanced at the man with the beard and moustache standing behind me. Why did I feel like I recognised him?

As we waited for the stage to be reset for the final illusion, I looked around me. It was very strange — I could roughly determine the shape of my front room, but the walls had all changed: they had become dark wood panels. The rugs and sofas had certainly disappeared — and where the wall with Alexander's poster had once been was the little stage. And the furniture was definitely new — well, old actually. It looked very much like pictures I'd seen of the Egyptian Hall, the astonishing little theatre of mystery that had once stood in London's Piccadilly and was long associated with David Devant.

✳

aster of Mystery

f performers, Devant started young. At the age
in 1878, he saw a travelling conjuror and was
ly hooked. He spent years learning everything he
and often visited the Egyptian Hall to see magicians
n, just like Servais Le Roy had done as a young man.
Hall was run as a magic theatre by the greatest of all
orian magicians, John Nevil Maskelyne, who offered
vant a job.

It's funny how Devant – born David Wighton – decided
his stage name. The story goes that he saw a picture in an
rt gallery, a biblical scene showing the fight between David
and Goliath. The title was 'David Devant Goliath' – 'devant'
being French for 'in front of'. Young Wighton obviously
thought it had a ring to it!

Anyway, Devant was a natural and soon carved a great reputation for himself as a first-class performer – full of wit and
charm. And he also invented loads of really amazing illusions.

He had a keen eye for knowing what magic wo[...]
the public, and as a result he became the be[...]
highest-paid magician of his day. Devant had[...]
inventiveness, artistry and an astute busine[...]

But one of the most interesting parts of[...]
to the greatest entertainment innovation [...]
the cinema. Devant was one of the first t[...]
a public audience in England – and he d[...]
of the Egyptian Hall. Describing the sho[...]
films as 'Animated Photographs', Devant i[...]
his magic shows. In those days people fou[...]
magical even without special effects. There's a[...]
about one of the first films to be shown in public[...]
It showed a train coming into view, and as the[...]
nearer and nearer, the audience literally jumped out[...]
seats, thinking that somehow the filmed train woul[...]
them over!

Devant was
friendly with
a Frenchman
by the name
of Georges
Méliès, who
made the first
ever sci-fi and
special-effect
films in a large

L ike a lot o
of ten,
immediatel
could – :
in actio
The
Vict
De

or
a

d appeal to

known and

ll: charisma,

d.

story tied him

Victorian age:

ilms in front of

n the tiny stage

black and white

cluded them in

nd films very

funny story

in France.

train got

of their

d run

glass conservatory built in the garden of his home. This was the first ever movie studio! He had started as a magician running Robert-Houdin's magic theatre in Paris, and sometimes presented Antonio Diavolo there – he owned the little acrobatic doll for a while. One of the very first films he ever made was of his friend David Devant pulling rabbits out of a hat. In those days films had to be made using daylight as there were no electrical lights strong enough for the job, so the magician was filmed standing on the roof of a theatre in London!

Devant saw that films were of great appeal to the public, but his boss at the Egyptian Hall, Maskelyne, wasn't convinced – he thought they were a passing fad. (Bet he kicked himself later.) So it was Devant who paid for the equipment and showed 'Animated Photographs'. He made a fortune with them, travelling around the country. He also bought some early film projectors and hired them out to other people at great cost.

Of course it was ironic – a strange twist of fate – that Devant and his fellow magicians who helped to fan the flames of the film industry didn't realise that they had made their own Frankenstein's monster. By the end of the 1920s, film had become so popular that places of live entertainment were closing down. It was the success of cinema that eventually led to the closing of all the variety theatres, such as the Hackney Empire, that magicians worked in.

But aside from film, Devant's achievements in magic were

phenomenal. He appeared in the first ever Royal Command performance, producing hundreds of eggs out of the air. The poor child helping him tried to hold them all, but they kept falling on the stage and smashing. The act caused a sensation! He also became the first president of the Magic Circle, the most famous magicians' society in the world, although many years later he was thrown out for explaining in a popular magazine how some of his own illusions were done.

The Maskelyne family had been forced out of the Egyptian Hall in 1904 (they'd been there for twenty-eight years) and set up another magic theatre in London – St George's Hall, in Langham Place, Upper Regent Street. They got into trouble very quickly. The opening production was a magic-based play called *The Coming Race* which just didn't sell many tickets. The Maskelynes were losing so much money that they had to do something to pull in the crowds – and quick! So they per-suaded Devant to come back off tour to pull in the punters again, and he was asked to become a business partner – he'd proved to be pretty smart with his animated pictures. Devant helped to make the St George's Hall magic theatre a huge suc-cess. It ran for another twenty-eight years and closed in 1933.

Maskelyne and Devant became household names, and between them were the greatest pioneers of magic the world has ever known. Maskelyne died in 1917, at the age of seventy-seven. Sadly, Devant had to retire at a relatively young age, suffering from an incurable illness, and spent many years in the Putney Home for Incurables in south-west London.

Every year, members of the Magic Circle would go there and put on a magic show for him. He died in 1941.

✳

As I was daydreaming about the heyday of English magic, the curtains swept back again. On the stage, roughly where the mirror had been in the scene before, was a large wooden crate. It must have been the size of an ordinary car, but with much higher sides – about the height of a bus shelter, I thought. The crate was open at one end and supported on wooden blocks so that I could see clear through underneath. Devant walked on to the stage, as charming as ever, and proceeded to bash the box on the front and back, walking and stamping inside it, to prove that the crate was indeed solid.

He then stepped out of the giant wooden case and picked up a small lamp on an electrical cable. It was not switched on. He moved to the front of the stage and dramatically held up his hand.

'Ladies and gentlemen,' he announced, 'I pray your fullest attention. In my hand is not just a normal electrical light. It is in fact a death ray – a death ray of enormous potential destructive power. It is fortunate that someone responsible is in charge of it – myself.'

He paused for dramatic effect, and then said, 'And now for the surprise.'

From the wings came the most ear-splitting noise – it

sounded like a badly tuned engine, and sure enough a man drove on to the stage from the side, perched on a little motor-cycle. He wore a funny chequered hat and goggles.

'May I present – Biff!' Devant exclaimed.

The driver drove around a couple of times in tight circles. I coughed from the smoke – I didn't even like frying onions in my house, let alone motorcycle exhaust fumes. But I was too caught up in the excitement to really care.

After showing off as much as he could in such a tiny area, the cyclist stopped, but kept the engine running.

'Into the box!' Devant ordered. A ramp was positioned leading up to the giant crate, and the rider drove his little motorcycle up and into it. The assistants removed the ramp and closed the end door. Then the box was winched slowly into the air until it was hovering about a metre off the floor.

I could still hear the motorbike revving away inside the box. Devant had stepped to the front of the stage, the death ray in his hand. The room lights dimmed and Devant switched on the lamp. It had an eerie green glow. He played the light up and down on the floor. Although I suspected the death ray story was just part of Devant's dramatic presentation, I got ready to duck in case he swung the lamp towards the audience. No point in taking any chances.

But thankfully Devant was very careful to keep the ray skimming the ground, as he stepped to the side of the suspended crate.

And then suddenly he swung the lamp upwards towards the box. Instantly the motorcycle was silent and at exactly the same moment the crate seemed to dissolve – dozens of individual strips of wood came crashing down to the stage. The lights grew in intensity. All that was left was a pile of wood – the motorcycle and rider had completely vanished!

This really was sensational, and I imagined that just seeing a motorbike onstage in those days must have been a thrill for the audience.

I leaped to my feet, applauding loudly.

The curtains swept closed and I looked around. The ticket collector was smiling at me.

'So – what did you think?' he asked

'Fantastic – I mean – I never thought I'd get to see David Devant perform – especially not here! He is a true legend – an all-time great. I wonder if there might be any chance of meeting him? And how on earth was that done?'

The man smiled at me with a familiar smile, and then pulled away the beard and moustache he had been sporting until that moment. Standing in front of me was the unmistakable figure of David Devant! Before I had a chance to ask him how that was possible he stepped forward.

'As I said, young man, all done by kindness,' he laughed.

'Well, Mr Devant,' I stuttered, not really being sure what to think or to say. I really was overwhelmed.

'So I hear you are a keen student of magic,' Devant said in an encouraging way.

I nodded – lost for words. I'd seen other great performers, of course, but Devant was almost too much! What could I ask him? Finally some words came tumbling out of my mouth before I could stop them.

'How many tricks do you know? I must know over fifty!' I gabbled.

Devant looked at me quizzically. 'About eight, I should say.'

I looked at him, puzzled.

'That is,' he added, 'I know eight tricks extremely well, inside out, back to front – in my sleep. You do not need to know many more. The secret of being a great magician is to know how to do just a few things really well – learn them so you know everything about them. These are the ones you will perform all your life. Of course I have performed many more than eight tricks in my career – so I may be exaggerating a little – but you understand my point . . .'

I nodded – back to practice, practice, practice again. But now I had another question for him.

'How have you become such an amazingly famous and successful magician?'

Devant smiled warmly at me and sighed. 'Such a difficult

question to answer – I have been asked it dozens of times. But I'll tell you a few things that I know. Firstly I have always, always, treated my audience with respect. You know you see some performers who get people up on stage and they are rude to them, they make nasty jokes about them just to get a cheap laugh? Well, that I don't agree with – it's not necessary. If you ask someone to help you out, you should treat them with respect – they are your guest on the stage.'

I nodded in agreement.

'Secondly, don't be afraid to put a story around your magic. You remember the lesson that Robert-Houdin gave you – that a magician is really an actor playing the part of a magician? Well, I'd go a bit further than that. A *great* magician is an actor playing the part of a magician. You often see magicians who don't act the role – they'll never be as good as some of the others you've seen here. A magician should create a fairy tale and then lead his audience to believe in it. That way they will be pleasantly deceived – they will feel wonder, not annoyance! Never be tempted to be a clever-clogs with your magic. Remember it is something to share with your audience, not to put yourself above them.'

He smiled again.

'And another thing – don't get too tied up with sleight of hand. Now, it's important – but don't do it just for the sake of it. It is only a means to an end – and the end is the strongest and most enjoyable magic effect for the audience. There's no point in practising a sleight-of-hand move for eighteen hours a day, seven days a week if the audience is neither mystified nor entertained by it!'

I was nodding again. Everything he said made perfect sense.

Devant added, 'What more can I say? I could write a book on the subject – oh, as a matter of fact I have.' He reached into his jacket and produced a hefty-looking volume. Where could he have been hiding it? There didn't seem to be enough room in his slimline jacket.

On the front of the book was a picture of a very old-looking wizard holding a steaming bowl of soup – or maybe it was a potion? He had a long white beard and wore a pointy hat with mysterious symbols on it. On the right-hand side of the picture were the words: *Our Magic – The Art in Magic, The Theory of Magic, The Practice of Magic by Nevil Maskelyne and David Devant.* (Nevil was the son of John Nevil, the co-founder of the Egyptian Hall.) The great magician handed it to me.

'Here,' he said. 'This contains all of my thoughts, together with those of my friend Nevil. This will keep you going for a long time – and if you get to the end, you'll be able to teach goldfish how to spell words, and a great deal besides.'

He handed me the book.

This was very generous of him. 'Thank you so much,' I said appreciatively. 'I promise I'll study it.' Then I plucked up the nerve to ask, 'But is there anything you can teach me now?'

'Well,' he said, 'there is something – but I must be quick. I have to set up my show for my special matinee performance.'

The Shy Coin

Devant took out of his pocket a tumbler, a coin and a sheet of newspaper. Again, I don't know how he fitted them all in!

He put the glass and newspaper down on the table by the wall and held up the coin. It was an old English penny (have you ever seen one? Big round thing, bigger than a 50p coin). He announced, 'I have become a circus master for ordinary household objects. I have taught forks how to walk on tightropes, handkerchiefs how to dance, plates how to swing on the trapeze. And this is my performing coin. It shows much promise and has been training for a while. Now you may wonder – what has it been learning?' With that he placed the coin on the table.

I realised that Devant was weaving his story. He was being an actor in order to lead me into the magic.

'Well, it has been learning to be a magical coin. It has been studying how to disappear in front of your eyes! The trouble is, the little coin is a bit shy. This, in fact, is her first perform-ance! So she has chosen to perform her vanishing act concealed by a piece of newspaper, but so that we can still hear her, a fellow student has also volunteered.' Devant picked up the drinking beaker and placed it upside down over the coin now resting in the centre of the table. He rapidly slid the glass back and forth across the table top and the coin rattled inside it. 'So now I will cover the glass and coin with the newspaper –' Devant scrunched the paper around the glass – 'so now the shy coin can disappear under the cover of the newspaper and the glass.'

Devant rattled the glass from side to side again. 'One, two, three,' he said, and immediately lifted the newspaper-covered glass away. The coin was still on the table.

'Oh dear,' he said. 'Never mind – it must be first-time nerves.'

He covered the coin again, and again shook the glass from side to side, making the coin rattle about.

'One, two, three!' he said once more, quickly lifting the glass – but the coin still just sat there. Devant looked at it encouragingly, covering the coin once again with the glass wrapped in the newspaper. 'Oh dear, poor thing. Some of my students learn quicker than others,' he said – and as he spoke he slammed his hand down on top of the newspaper. It flattened completely against the table top. The glass itself had completely vanished!

'I forgot to mention,' he said with a broad smile. 'The glass was a much quicker student.' And he reached under the table and retrieved the glass. 'It has learned how to pass through a solid table top!'

I was astonished.

Devant looked at me with a serious expression on his face. 'Now, you do know that you should not reveal the secrets of magic other than to those who are seriously practising the art?' he asked me, and I nodded. 'Well, then,' he said, 'I will show you this as a serious student.

'Now I demonstrated this with a glass, but why don't you use that funny-looking cup?' He pointed to a plastic goblet I had placed on the shelf by the window. It was colourful with straight sides. Devant tapped it with his fingers. 'That looks perfect! It won't smash if it falls on the floor! You'll also need a sheet of newspaper and a coin. You will notice how I told you a story to build up the magic – it was a little fairy tale, and you were drawn into the story. I wasn't showing you a demonstration of "Aren't I clever?" – I was sharing with you a charming little tale of my unusual students! So at the end you should be baffled – but baffled in a charmed sort of a way.

'Well, this is a good lesson in misdirection.'

I remembered that word from Robert-Houdin's lesson on the invisible card.

'You take the beaker and invert it – turn it upside down – over the coin. That way, when you rattle it you can hear the penny (although you can use any of your modern coins). Draw the audience's attention to the coin. When you wrap the newspaper around the beaker, it will naturally form the same shape. And here lies the secret!

'You have to perform this sitting at a table. Your spectators should be sitting opposite you. Get them to fix their attention on the coin and then cover the coin with the beaker, then cover all with the newspaper. Rattle the coin so that the audience can hear it. Tell the audience your story – that the coin will disappear. Lift the newspaper-covered tumbler in the air. The coin will still be there. Act a little disappointed, and then cover the coin again. Rattle rattle. Lift the beaker again – the coin is still there. But unknown to the spectator, this time you have let the tumbler fall out of the newspaper cover and into

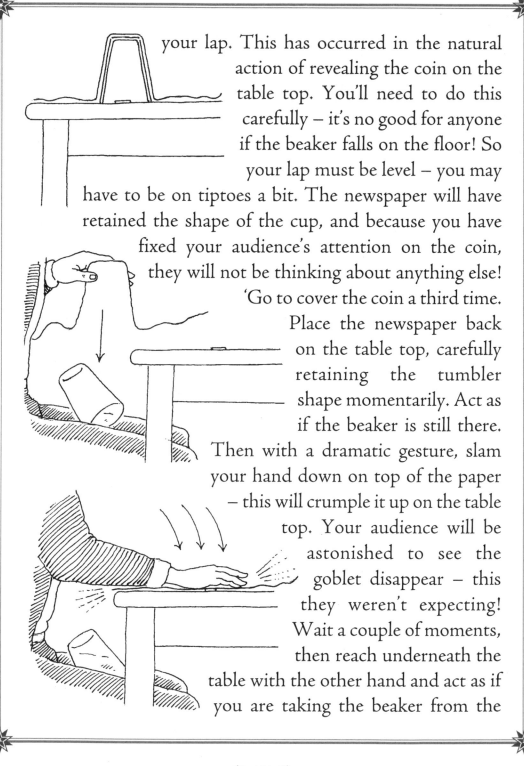

your lap. This has occurred in the natural action of revealing the coin on the table top. You'll need to do this carefully – it's no good for anyone if the beaker falls on the floor! So your lap must be level – you may have to be on tiptoes a bit. The newspaper will have retained the shape of the cup, and because you have fixed your audience's attention on the coin, they will not be thinking about anything else! 'Go to cover the coin a third time. Place the newspaper back on the table top, carefully retaining the tumbler shape momentarily. Act as if the beaker is still there. Then with a dramatic gesture, slam your hand down on top of the paper – this will crumple it up on the table top. Your audience will be astonished to see the goblet disappear – this they weren't expecting! Wait a couple of moments, then reach underneath the table with the other hand and act as if you are taking the beaker from the underside of the table. As you pass your hand past your lap, pick up the beaker from it, and then lift it up above the level of the table, showing it to your audience. They will be amazed that it appears to have passed through the solid table top!'

I was very impressed. I now understood how the illusion worked – fixing the audience's attention on to the coin was really a very powerful misdirection to what happened to the tumbler.

Devant stretched his arms above his head. 'You know, young man, I really fancy a spot of tea,' he said.

'No problem at all,' I said, suddenly remembering the chaos in my kitchen. 'I'll pop the kettle on.'

I left Devant sitting at the table and glanced once more around the room. I walked into the kitchen and switched the kettle on, smiling to myself – making tea for David Devant! I didn't want to waste a second of time with the master, so I left the kettle to boil (half wondering what strange liquids would emerge this time) and headed back along the hall. To my surprise the door of the Poster Room was shut again and once more a little note was hanging on the back of it. I looked at it closely – it read:

Dont forget to do it with kindness.
Yours
DD

I pushed the handle on the door and it swung open to reveal the room exactly as it normally was – no little stage, no wooden chairs. The posters were back on the wall and David Devant was nowhere to be seen.

Chapter 7

The Incredible Chinese Conjuror

FOR QUITE A FEW WEEKS I hadn't heard a magical squeak from any master magicians, but I had discovered the occasional imp in unexpected places. Little devils – they get everywhere. I'd found one asleep in a shoe in my bedroom, and another one snoozing in the airing cupboard beneath a pile of towels (I started to wonder if I could buy imp repellent in the supermarket . . .). One day I caught a particularly plump-looking beast stuffing its

face in the fridge. I was pretty certain it had escaped from Kellar's poster – I'd noticed that one of the imps perched on his shoulder seemed to be getting much larger as my supply of chocolate biscuits had been getting mysteriously smaller. Turned out I was right – after I'd chased it back into its poster with a fly swat, everything seemed peaceful once again.

I'd been practising quite a bit for my forthcoming theatre show, even though I hadn't had confirmation of the date yet from the Around Eightieth Agency. Once or twice I'd picked up the letter and looked at it, wondering when I would get more details, but there was no phone number on it to check. It stated clearly: *This is a definite booking* – and I wasn't going to argue. The chance to perform in a proper theatre would be amazing and I just had to he ready for the occasion whenever it was. But one evening I realised what with the rehearsing, materialising magicians and imp impositions, I hadn't done anything 'normal' in ages. *Time to relax*, I thought. *I'll chill out this evening with a DVD and a takeaway.*

So I ordered a feast from Hackney's finest Chinese and went to the Poster Room to set up my projector screen. I'd not used it for months – not since my magical manifestations had begun. I'd almost forgotten about it, in fact. When the screen is rolled up and out of the way, you'd never know it was there, hidden right above a big poster of Chung Ling Soo. But when I needed it – hey presto – home cinema!

I'd never given it a second thought before, but as I lowered the screen this time I wondered if Soo would take kindly to being covered over. After all, he wasn't known for being in the background – he'd made his name by making sure he was always the one in front of his competitors! As I pulled the screen downwards, I could have sworn that the magician's face looked even sterner than usual. *Oh, it'll be fine,* I thought, *I'll watch* Edward Scissorhands. *He won't see Edward as competition – he's not known for his sleight of hand (and as for Edward doing card tricks – that's a recipe for instant confetti!).*

Then, as I was slightly uneasily sorting through my DVD collection, trying to find it, I heard a sudden bang. The takeaway, maybe? Seemed very quick. But when I opened the door, nobody was there. It must have been a noise in the street.

Back in my home cinema space, I set up the projector on a table opposite the screen. I had to move a few things out of the way to avoid unwanted shadows, like a Chinese vase I'd bought from an antique shop up the road a while back. It was decorated with fantastical blue and white dragons, and seemed a good idea at the time because it reminded me of the design of the rice bowls in my first magic set. But now it was always getting in the way and didn't seem to be serving any kind of useful purpose – so I'd stuck a rather sad-looking pot plant in it the week before.

By the time I'd found the film and loaded it into the player, the takeaway really had arrived. I dimmed the lights, settled back on my sofa, chopsticks in one hand, remote control in the other. Up came the credits and in went the food. Perfect!

But I should have known to expect the unexpected. Before long, there was another bang even louder than the one before. This was followed by a whole series of little crashes, drilling noises and muffled shouts. Although my uneasiness was growing I was determined not to be distracted, so I turned up the volume a couple more notches and stared at the screen.

BANG . . . CRASH – then the sound of more muffled shouting. *This really can't be right*, I thought. I knew this was-n't on the normal soundtrack. And I couldn't imagine they'd be digging up the road at this time in the evening. A distinct feeling was creeping up on me that I wasn't going to get to the end of this film . . .

Then one minute I was looking at Johnny Depp snapping his shears in the air, the next minute the image was going crazy. It seemed to be swirling around like the pattern on my Chinese vase – what was going on? Was something wrong with my state-of-the-art video projector?

'The boss wants that cleaned AGAIN!' I heard someone bellowing. I nearly jumped out of my skin – the voice was louder than the movie soundtrack, and there was no one else in the room or in the garden. What was going on? Then I realised – the sounds weren't coming from outside the house but from *behind* the screen, and the distortions on the film were partly being caused by someone or something knocking into the back of it – which was impossible because the screen was flat against the poster. But then by now I knew that the impossible wasn't out of the question at all.

So much for a quiet evening in, I thought . . . on the other hand, if this magical visitor was who I thought it was, it'd be a dream come true!

Putting down my takeaway tray, I tiptoed to the screen, and cautiously lifted up one end of it — just enough to be able to peer beneath. What I saw made me gasp.

Behind it I could see the battered floorboards of an old wooden stage, with feet shuffling about. Poking my head further in and looking up, I saw that they belonged to workmen dressed in funny old clothes, busily sawing wood, winding wires around wooden blocks and dashing around, while one of them stood to the side with a clipboard, making notes. The stage was covered in battered-looking crates. Lots of assistants were carefully unpacking them, unrolling Chinese carpets and banners and polishing elaborate pieces of exotic-looking oriental apparatus.

One of them caught sight of me. 'Oi!' he hissed. 'We're not

ready yet! Curtain's not due up for half an hour! Don't let Mr Soo catch you poking your nose in here – he'll turn you into crispy duck.' And he grabbed the screen from the other side and snapped it shut again. Strangely his side of the screen looked like it was made of deep red velvet.

I backed hurriedly to my sofa, expecting to see the swirling film again – but hang on a minute! It wasn't a screen any more but an old theatre curtain. A thrill of anticipation went through me. Of all the magicians I had ever wanted to see . . .

Mr Soo. Chung Ling Soo. So I'd been right when I thought he wouldn't like being hidden away! This was going to beat any movie for sure.

I picked up the takeaway again. Not that I felt hungry now – just very excited. I was about to watch one of the greatest magicians in his-tory perform his celebrated illusions.

I pushed the last of my mushrooms (now slightly con-gealed) around with my chopsticks. I couldn't catch one particularly slippery specimen, so grabbed it tightly between my thumb and forefinger. Just before I got it to my mouth it pinged away across the room at great speed, striking the cur-tain and landing on the floor with a plop. *Not as dangerous as some of the objects fired at Soo during his show*, I thought to myself!

Chinese Whispers

Even today, Chung Ling Soo is admired by magicians all round the world – for his showmanship, certainly, but mostly for his amazing magical inventions. He was a truly brilliant magician, obsessed with dreaming up wizardry that not only astonished and baffled his audience, but his fellow conjurors too.

Soo became one of the greatest stars of the golden age of magic. He'd started young, performing his first show at the age of fourteen in 1875, and worked as an assistant to some of the great magicians of his time. By the early years of the twentieth century he was an international sensation, playing in the largest and most famous of theatres and earning a fortune wherever he went.

From the moment he stepped on to the stage, Soo thrilled audiences with his exotic appearance – dressed in a gorgeous Chinese embroidered robe with sweeping sleeves, his hair pulled back into a long, thin plait. Mind you, Soo's tricks would have been a hit if he was wearing baggy shorts and flippers. He dazzled audiences with sensational illusions, such as conjuring up from a silk scarf a huge bowl filled to the brim with water and real ducks. From a boiling bubbling fiery cauldron he would pull live chickens, doves – and then his wife! His magic defied belief . . .

Defied death, too. As a climax to some of his shows, two of his assistants fired a bullet at him from two muzzle-loading muskets (a kind of old-fashioned rifle where the bullets and gunpowder are rammed down the barrel). The bullets (which looked like lead marbles) would have been specially marked by members of the audience so they could identify them again.

Then Soo would stand with a small china plate clasped in front of his chest. *Bang!* would go the rifles, Soo would stagger back for a nail-biting moment, and then *plink!* went the bullets as he displayed them rolling around the plate. The audience members would immediately check that their marked bullets were the same as those loaded into the guns. It was a mystery that became world famous.

Of course, no one can really catch a bullet no matter how great a magician they are! Nevertheless, the illusion was a very dangerous one – at least ten other people had been killed trying to perform versions of it. Even daring performers of the time, such as Houdini, never attempted the feat, fearing it was too dangerous. But Soo, with his secret method that completely foxed other magicians, created a sensation wherever he went. He seemed to have a truly 'bullet-proof' way of doing the sensational stunt. Some people wondered if his secret would ever be known as he survived unscathed for years on end.

Tragically, though, Soo couldn't defy death for ever.

On Saturday, 23 March 1918, he was performing to a packed house in London's Wood Green Empire. The First World War was still going on, and people flocked to see variety shows to take their minds off things.

Soo had already performed a wonderfully spectacular series of illusions and was nearing the dramatic climax of the show. Drums rolled as Soo stood upright, holding the china plate. The assistants loaded their rifles, ramming bullet and gunpowder down the muzzles, all under the close inspection of the volunteers from the audience. (As this was during the war, the volunteers could well have been soldiers on leave. They would have been familiar with guns and bullets, and would have known if there was anything dodgy about them — this all helped to make the illusion more authentic.) The two assistants took aim. Fire!

And he staggered back, crying out. He dropped the plate and fell to the ground. Something had gone horribly wrong. He was taken to hospital, but by Sunday morning Chung Ling Soo was dead. It was sensational news and made the headlines of all the daily newspapers — my grandfather was still talking about it when I was a kid.

So what did go wrong?

The papers were full of speculation: had someone

tampered with the guns and murdered him? (His private life was rather shady.) Or had Soo committed suicide because he was in debt?

It turned out to be a tragic accident, caused by a fatal flaw in one of the guns. Both of them had been cleverly adapted to have two barrels very close to each other. The real gunpowder and bullet were put in one barrel, which was never meant to be fired, and only blanks placed in the other. The gun was supposed to operate like a toy cap gun, making a loud noise but never shooting anything out of it. But over the years tiny grains of gunpowder had gradually leaked between the cylinders. On the fateful night, there was just enough powder to connect the blank cylinder to the real one, and the blank charge had accidentally set off both – firing out the lead ball and fatally wounding the great magician.

He would have secretly palmed the two marked bullets, holding them behind the china plate. As he collapsed to the floor in his final performance, they would have fallen from his hand. No one would have noticed them as the plate shattered on the wooden stage and Chung Ling Soo lay on the floor, bleeding.

What a tragic end to a great career, I thought, still sitting on my sofa. The remaining Chinese mushrooms had grown cold, so I put the foil dishes on the floor.

Hmmm – Chinese. It was funny (well, not funny – odd as well as sad) that in his final appearance Soo actually cried out. He always performed in silence, with an assistant introducing the acts. It added to his air of inscrutable oriental mystery. But on that fateful night, the first and last words he ever spoke in front of an audience were, 'Oh my god. Something's happened. Lower the curtain!' In English!

So Chung Ling Soo practised illusions in real life too. Just as I was thinking this over, the lights in the room grew dimmer . . .

✳

The old curtains swept open, revealing a tiny lady in elaborate Chinese dress, standing in a spotlight. I knew she must be Suee Seen, Soo's wife, who worked as his assistant.

Suee gestured to a tall, elegant glass cabinet behind her. It was mounted on small wheels, and assistants turned it all the way round, showing it had six identical transparent sides. Suee then took a flaming torch from an assistant and opened a door in one of the panels, shining the light inside to show that it was empty. She then circled round the cabinet, illuminating each side in turn.

No way was anything or anybody in that cabinet!

A couple of cables came down from above. Assistants quickly tied them on to a metal ring fixed to the top. Suee waved her hand, and the cabinet rose a few feet into the air, swinging gently. She then tossed her torch aside, grabbed one side of the frame and started to spin it round. It rotated quickly, reflecting the stage lights as it spun.

I sat hypnotised, unable to take my eyes off the twirling crystal box. I could see through the shimmering lights that the giant lantern was still empty.

Suddenly, Suee clapped her hands and there was a sharp noise that made me jump. It seemed to be coming from one side of the room. Out of the corner of my eye I could see my Chinese vase, vibrating madly. Then – *phut!* A little firework explosion ejected my plant a couple of feet in the air. It fell on to the floor, looking decidedly scorched.

Then all was silent again. *That must be a signal*, I thought – *but for what?*

As I stared at the cabinet, a weird thing started to happen. Colours were gradually swimming into view through the spinning sides. They became brighter and brighter, and as the spinning began to slow down, I couldn't believe what I was seeing. Somehow the patterns of colour seemed to form themselves into the hands and face of a man – who for a moment seemed still as the cabinet revolved. The next moment the figure was spinning quickly inside. But in the instant it had been still, I recognised who it was. It was the great Chung Ling Soo himself!

The cabinet was now lowered to the floor. As it came to a stop, Suee and another assistant steadied it, and Soo stepped out, dressed in his trademark elaborate Chinese robe, a long plait over one shoulder. He bowed deeply, hands buried in his long flowing sleeves. It really seemed as if he had materialised from nowhere. I'd read about this illusion in my books – it was called 'The Crystal Lamp of Enchantment' – but I never thought I'd get to see it.

I rose to my feet in excitement. 'That was amazing!' I cried – and I really meant it. 'Bravo!' I applauded till my hands were sore. Once I'd stopped clapping I suddenly became conscious that my magical idol might catch sight of my untidy Chinese takeaway containers and I tried pushing them under the sofa with my foot. One of them fell over with a clatter, ejecting a half-eaten bit of chicken towards the stage. I pretended not to notice.

Chung Ling Soo bowed again, keeping his customary dignified silence, while his assistants busily cleared the stage behind him.

Little Suee Seen stepped forward while mysterious Chinese music filled the air.

'And now,' she announced, 'the marvellous Chinese conjuror, Chung Ling Soo, will present to you a spectacular feast of wonders!'

The great magician bowed once more, wearing the inscrutable expression I recognised from the poster. He stepped back and took up a position behind a wide table draped in colourful Chinese fabric, on top of which was an assortment of exotic-looking objects.

Soo picked up a soup plate, showing both sides, took a handful of what looked like birdseed from a jar, and sprinkled it into the plate. He then took another soup plate, again showing both sides, and placed it over the first one, upside down. The magician passed his hands several times over the two plates and pushed his wide sleeves back. Then with a flourish he lifted up the top plate – and a beautiful white dove flew out! I applauded politely. But he was only warming up.

An assistant brought a large bowl filled with what looked like cotton wool. Soo pushed back his sleeves again, plunged his hands into the bowl and started to eat the cotton wool, stuffing it into his mouth. At first I thought it was candy floss, but when I looked closely I could see it was real cotton wool for sure (yuk!). *Not one to try at home*, I thought.

When he'd stuffed loads of it in, he started pulling things out of his mouth – metres and metres of ribbons of all colours, and then – how bizarre – an old-fashioned red-and-white-striped barber's pole. Then he gathered up the ribbons, twisted them in his hands – and next minute he was holding a Chinese-style paper umbrella! *Well, he must have the biggest mouth in the world*, I thought – surprising for someone who didn't say much!

I applauded like mad. I have to say I always felt a bit self-conscious clapping loudly when I was the only one in the room, but I couldn't help myself. I was enthralled. Watching Soo also made me think how many more effects you have to do when you perform in silence – you can't take up time with funny patter and magic words.

Assistants brought in a number of round glass bowls full of water and put them on the table. Suee gave Soo a fishing rod and line, and he flicked it about near him, as if he was

practising casting. With another flourish he cast the line far into the room and swung it around alarmingly close to my nose. Then right on the end I could see a little orange thing wriggling about – he had caught a goldfish from just above my right ear! Where could that have come from? He quickly reeled in the line and released the fish into one of the bowls, where it swam about quite happily. (If it's true that goldfish have a very short attention span, perhaps it'd already forgotten how it got there.)

Soo repeated this very impressive illusion several times, apparently catching fish from mid-air around the room, till all the bowls were full. I hoped he'd caught them all and that there were no more goldfish swimming around invisibly in the house – I wouldn't like to wake up and find one in my mouth.

Now the atmosphere changed: the lights dimmed further and a drum began to beat. I hoped Soo wouldn't try his ill-fated bullet-catching here – I didn't think my first-aid kit was sufficiently equipped – but I needn't have worried. Instead of a musket, he used . . . an enormous old-fashioned black iron cannon! That's all right, then, GULP!

The menacing-looking thing was dragged on to the stage, and Soo swung it round so that its mouth was pointing straight at me.

Wait a minute . . . imagining my state-of-the-art projector being blown to bits (never mind me), I hurriedly moved the table out of the firing range, grinning nervously at the great magician and trying to look like I trusted him. I stood to one side, wondering if my household insurance covered things like damage from an old magician's lethal-looking big gun. He seemed very confident, I thought, but I probably knew more about his history with gunpowder than he did!

Soo helped his tiny wife, Suee, into the cannon's barrel – she disappeared right inside it. He then picked up a large, black cannonball from the floor, staggering a little under the weight, and placed it into the barrel too (I hoped it wouldn't squash Suee). With another of his elegant flour-ishes he then blew some fire out of his mouth and lit a taper (no wonder he did-n't speak onstage – he'd be setting fire to things all the time). He lit the fuse with the taper. I put my hands over my ears.

Bang! The cannonball shot out right to the end of the room and hit the wall, where it just disintegrated in a puff of smoke. I watched as the smoke cleared (very relieved that I still had a wall) and then saw Suee Seen standing there just underneath, smiling and bowing!

In a huge theatre she must have appeared right at the back

of the seats, which would have been even more amazing. Suee walked elegantly back through the room, bowing as she went, and handed me a little postcard of Chung Ling Soo as a souvenir. I thanked her and placed it carefully on to the chair beside me. The card showed Soo in Chinese armour, holding a willow-pattern plate in front of him – his outfit for the bullet-catching trick.

I was enthralled. The illusions themselves were incredible, but the way Soo performed them – one after the other, with hardly a break – built up a magical kaleidoscope that took my breath away.

I walked hesitantly towards Soo, who was standing aloof while his assistants were clearing the stage behind him and sweeping up stuff from the floor.

'That was fantastic!' I said. 'It was beautiful, amazing. Will you be performing any more? Your bullet-catch, perhaps?'

He looked at me with a slight sneer and glanced at Suee, who was now by his side.

'The master does not understand your words,' little Suee sang out. 'I shall translate for you.'

Suee took a deep breath and started uttering some strange words, which sounded very vaguely like Chinese. But I'd often heard my Chinese neighbours next door, chatting to each other in their back garden, and they never talked like this.

I realised I had to say what I knew.

I interrupted nervously. 'Er – er, it's very nice to welcome you to my home, Billy.' I knew he spoke English as well as

I did. He was as authentically Chinese as my Hackney takeaway!

Yes – remember his dying words? English. With an American accent, that is. Now I can tell you that the great Chung Ling Soo had been born William Ellsworth Robinson, in New York City, USA. For much of his professional life he carried off his Chinese impersonation both onstage and in real life. When required to speak Chinese in public, he would have got away with gobbledegook – few people at the time were familiar with the language and most wouldn't have known he was faking it. (Apart from his main competitor, that is, a real Chinese magician called Ching Ling Foo – and Soo had the nerve to say that Foo was the copy!)

But he was offstage now, and I knew his biggest secret (and I suppose a lot of other people did at the time, though they didn't let on to the public). I hoped we might be able to talk, one magician to another, as long as he wasn't offended.

Soo – or Billy – was frowning heavily at me. Suee was fluttering nervously at his side. (I knew that she too was no more Chinese than her husband – a girl from Kentucky, nicknamed Dot as she was so small.) The more he glared at me the more uncomfortable I felt. What if the magic history books had been wrong and I had gravely offended him? Perhaps he would turn me into crispy duck after all!

No – I felt sure I was right. I had just read a whole book all about his life in the US.

I nervously smiled at him. 'I'm honoured to have you in my

home, sir. I've always admired your work – you're one of the greatest magicians of all time. I could really learn from you.'

(And I wasn't saying that just to get round him – I really meant it.)

My guest seemed to unbend a little, then, in a New York accent, he growled, 'I guess it wouldn't hurt to step out of character for a while. Under the circumstances. Hey – I've not been to Hackney for all of ninety-six years, pal!' And he slapped me on the back rather firmly. It seemed that Chung Ling Soo had transformed into Billy Robinson.

I breathed a sigh of relief – and so did Suee/Dot.

Now he'd relaxed, Billy was more than happy to show me how to do one of his illusions – a really good one.

He was sitting on my sofa, Dot standing next to him (like this, they were almost the same height!). His assistants had arranged themselves tidily on the floor in front of the stage curtain, which was now pulled shut again. They sat quietly and patiently; Soo must have run a tight ship.

✺

The Chinese Paper Mystery

Billy (I couldn't think of him as Soo when he was actually talking in an American accent!) stood up and announced, 'This is a routine I used to do way back – when I used to talk!' He grinned. 'I'd tell the audience a story. I'd tell them that in ancient China there was a blade so sharp that it could cut through things without leaving a mark. There was a legend that if a great warrior swung this sword quickly enough, it could pass through solid trees without cutting them down!

'Well, it'd be too dangerous to wave a sharp sword here – and we'd never get a tree into this room. But I can show you just what I mean by using scissors and a piece of paper.'

He turned to his wife. 'Would you mind, Dot?'

She nipped behind the curtain and returned a few moments later with a long strip of beautiful oriental paper and a pair of scissors.

Taking them from her, Billy held them up and declared, 'I'd like to show you the Chinese Paper Mystery. Now, these scissors are made from the same metal as the ancient warrior's sword –' he had a glint in his eye and I could see he was enjoying the acting! – 'and the paper, after all, comes from a tree.'

Billy had now folded the paper loosely in half. 'Now, if I was using normal scissors, you'd imagine that if I cut off a piece from the middle of the paper –' and he did so, the cut-off strip falling to the floor – 'that I would now have two pieces in my hand. Well, not so – the Chinese scissors have cut through without harm.'

He had clearly cut a piece from the middle of the paper, but he now allowed the paper to fall open again – showing that amazingly the paper was still in one strip.

'You may wonder if this is always so,' Billy continued. 'Well, it would only work for the ancient warrior if the cut was made in a straight line. If he hit the tree at an angle, a very strange thing would happen to the tree!' As he spoke, he folded the long strip of paper in half once again, but this time he cut across the strip at an angle.

He flicked the paper open. 'See what I mean?' Now it was not one long strip, but bent in the middle, a bit like a partially straightened-out letter 'L'. But it was still in one piece! My mouth fell open – surely it wasn't possible? It was as if the paper was fusing itself back together as soon as it was cut.

Billy was continuing his act. 'And that would take some powerful magic to straighten out – particularly on a tree.' He cut off a strip from the centre of the paper once again and it fell to the floor. Then he flicked out the whole strip of paper – and it was now restored back into one piece!

A classic bit of magic! Billy took a small bow as we all clapped, and I hoped he would teach me his amazing oriental mystery.

After the applause died down, Dot took the scissors back from him and then started scrambling on the floor to clear up the bits of paper that had been cut away.

'Oh, don't worry about that,' I said to her. 'I can do that later.' She stood back up and gave a delicate bow.

Billy walked over to me and said, 'Well now, I'm happy to show you how to perform it – it would be my pleasure. But remember it is a precious secret!'

Great!

'I used fancy paper,' he said, 'but I guess ordinary old news-paper works just as well. You need a strip about this long –' he held his hands apart, about the length of the long side of a normal big newspaper – 'and you'll need some rubbery glue.'

'Ah,' I said, 'that'd be cow gum, or Copydex. You can buy it in stationery shops.' I'd heard it referred to as rubber cement.

'Whatever,' said Billy. 'You gotta spread the stuff on one side of the newspaper. Spread it carefully and thinly, and cover around the centre third of the newspaper strip. Here – I'll show you.' And with that he took out a little pot of glue and some more strips of paper to demonstrate.

'Allow it to dry

completely,' Billy went on. 'Next, get some talcum powder and shake it on to the glued side of the newspaper, and shake it off. This stops the stuff sticking to itself too early.

'When you come to do your magic show, you take the pre-pared newspaper and fold it over in half, so that the glued and powdered surface is on the inside of the fold facing itself. Now cut straight across the end of the newspaper with a pair of scissors – with me so far?' he asked.

'It looks straightforward enough. I hope I remember the details though.'

'Don't worry,' he said. He reached into his robe and took out a pencil and a piece of notepaper. Useful places to store things, those elaborate robes. He made a few sketches and went on describing the trick.

'Now hold one end of the paper and allow the whole strip to unfold. The paper appears to be in one piece! In actual fact it's not, and if you pulled gently on both ends it'd fall into two pieces. But the glue has been pressed together just where the scissors cut – and this holds the paper together just enough for you to show it as restored.'

So that's the secret!

Billy hadn't finished. 'Try cutting the paper at a different angle, keeping the cut in a straight line. When you open it up, the paper will come out in a funny L shape, just like in the sketch. You can cut the paper two or three times, and provided you don't run out of the glued section you prepared, the glue will stick to itself and hold the paper together, as I said – provided the cut is always made in a straight line.'

'That's wonderful,' I said. 'I can't thank you enough.'

'Aw, don't mention it,' said Billy.

And with that, the friendly New Yorker disappeared and the serious Chinese man was back. Billy was Chung Ling Soo once more, as if he had never dropped his mask.

Soo bowed to me, I bowed back, then he spun around with a swirl of his colourful robe and marched off behind the curtain. Suee trotted after him and, one by one, the assistants followed.

Just as the last man disappeared there was another sudden *CRACKLE!* that made me jump. I glanced over at the vase – it was vibrating again as if a whole lot of firecrackers were going off inside it. By now the scorched pot plant looked really sorry for itself, lying limply on the floor.

I'd only taken my eyes off the curtain for a moment, but when I looked back it had vanished. The screen was back in place, rolled up above the poster of Chung Ling Soo and company – just printed images again.

I stood for a moment, blinking at the poster. What a performance! And I couldn't wait to try out the Chinese Paper Mystery – I was so glad Billy had left his sketches.

First, though, I thought, *I'd just better clear the remains of my takeaway. I might even do the washing-up . . .*

Chapter 8

Goddess of Mystery

WHILE MY HOME WAS BECOMING increasingly like a mini Hackney Empire, I was trying to lead as normal a life as possible – which wasn't easy. In between the mayhem of my magical visitors there was the small matter of making a living, so I had to go to work meetings as usual and over Christmas I'd had a busy time performing magic at office parties to people who weren't always brilliantly behaved, so I was relieved that the holiday season was out of the way. And now it was the new year I was trying to catch up with friends once in a while too. I'd not really said anything to them about my mysterious guests – I didn't want them thinking that I was completely off my trolley. Most of my non-magician mates thought what I did was decidedly odd in any case. I'd sometimes tell them about some strange effect I was designing for a theatre production (like the one I was doing at the time – making a ballet-dancing Alice in Wonderland stretch to twice her normal height in the middle of a dance), and they'd look at me with a puzzled expression and say, 'How nice – have you ever thought of getting a proper job?' If I told them that I'd been visited by a procession of master magicians from long ago, it would be way too much for them.

Now you might think my magician friends would be more understanding. But I was worried that if I mentioned the goings-on to them, then half the Magic Circle would set up camp outside my house, hoping for a glimpse of one of the all-time greats.

Anyhow, every time I got home after being with friends or at meetings I'd open the front door very cautiously and peer into the hall. I'd quickly look in the front rooms, whiz upstairs and check the bedrooms, office and the bathroom (thankfully no one had yet materialised when I was in there!), then finally the Poster Room at the back of the house. I knew that room was the one most likely to spring surprises. If everything was quiet in there, I could relax – at least for a while. And bedtimes were normally OK. Nothing had happened at night. Yet . . .

One evening, I'd been to a meeting of ELMS (that's the East London Magical Society). We meet in this funny old hall a couple of miles from where I live. The walls are all panelled with dark wood, and the place is always terribly cold and musty-smelling (it's almost like someone has shoved a load of old socks behind the radiators – but there aren't any radiators). Still, it's a useful place for meetings. Different people speak about their magical experiences, some visiting magicians lecture about their latest ideas and magic effects, and we all go for a nice dinner afterwards.

This particular Monday had been a good one – I'd seen a few magical mates I hadn't seen for a long time, and I'd learned how to change a white handkerchief into an egg using pure sleight of hand. I was eggstatic!

When I got home, just after midnight, I went through the usual routine of checking for anything out of the ordinary. Thankfully, things seemed quiet around the house (I thought I'd seen quite enough magicians for one evening), and I finally arrived in the Poster Room and turned on the lights. No signs of activity. I walked round the room, gazing at each of the magicians in turn. They all seemed still and flat – not even the hint of a twitch. There hadn't been a squeak out of any of them since Chung Ling Soo had visited a couple of months back, just before Christmas. Perhaps they'd all finished with me. Though Alexander did say that I'd know for sure when my magical visitations were over . . .

Then I got to the small alcove at the back of the room. I'd reserved this space for a special poster, a very unusual one. Unusual because it was a poster advertising a lady magician – Ionia. Women did perform in magic shows, of course, but usually as assistants. They'd be levitated, sawn in half and placed in vanishing boxes. A few women did have routines of their own, like Talma, the Queen of Coins, who mainly worked with her husband, Servais Le Roy. Fewer still toured with their own troupe, and Ionia was one of them. It's still the same today – there are far more male magicians than female. I know that women and girls enjoy watching magic as much as men and boys, so why there aren't more female magicians is a mystery to me.

In a world dominated by magical males, Ionia certainly made her presence felt. She chose to describe herself as 'The Goddess of Mystery'. Even the greatest of the male magicians, with the hugest egos, never actually described themselves as gods – just 'supreme masters' of this, 'grand rulers' of that, 'world monarchs' of the other. Very modest in comparison!

I gazed at the poster of the goddess, raising her arms to the star-studded night sky, her shimmering gown studded with jewels and sequins, her beautiful face framed by clouds of dark hair and a circle of gold with a mystical symbol on her head. She certainly would have brought more than a touch of glamour as well as mystery to the stage!

As I was looking at Ionia's stunning poster, I remembered a conversation I'd had at dinner that evening. Some of the magicians who go to my club aren't known for their up-to-date view of the world (in fact a few of them need to be dragged kicking and screaming into the twentieth century, let alone the twenty-first). Anyway, I'd mentioned to this bloke sitting next to me that a friend of mine – a young woman – was just starting out in the magic business. He spluttered into his soup. 'Women!' he said. 'Women can't be magicians – they can't keep secrets!'

I'd argued with him, but it was no good. He was completely stuck with his silly attitude.

'Well, Goddess of Mystery,' I said out loud to Ionia's poster, 'what would you say to someone who thought women can't keep secrets? You must have kept quite a few in your time!'

I chuckled to myself and contemplated going off to bed,

when there was a snorting sound behind me. Uh-oh – what I'd said had obviously ruffled some feathers. I turned round slowly, wondering what I'd see.

Nothing, at first. Then suddenly just about every image on the posters started shifting about. It was like I'd lifted a rock off an ants' nest – they were all getting agitated. Alexander was the first to speak. He leaned out of his poster, shaking his head from side to side, his turban wobbling alarmingly. He had gone slightly red in the face.

'Women!' he sneered. 'Don't talk to me about women magicians. All they do is stand there and look pretty. What do they know about skills and techniques? They ain't got the brains. They're OK onstage if they're fetchin' and carryin', or singin' a song or doin' a dance. But performin' magic? Forget it!'

There was a chorus of 'Right!' and heads nodded all round, except on Le Roy's poster, where he and his wife, Talma, were frowning. And Devant was looking a bit sad and shaking his head from side to side.

'What about Talma?' I asked the room. 'She's a master performer.'

Alexander shifted his gaze to her. 'Well, OK, Talma's pretty good,' he said grudgingly, 'but she didn't get big ideas;

at least she mainly stayed in her husband's show. But that – that Ionia –' he coughed out her name as if he had eaten a bogey pie – 'she thought she had what it takes to be the star turn. She called herself a – a goddess!'

Now The Great Lafayette joined in, sounding even more spiteful. 'Ionia,' he said scornfully. 'My dog Beauty's more of a magician than she is! She just dressed herself up in a crazy mix of Egyptian and oriental costumes to look exotic. Didn't know what she was supposed to be. Calling herself Ionia – that wasn't even her real name. And it's Greek – what's that got to do with the Orient?'

Hmm, I thought – *dressing up and changing your name. That's rich coming from you.*

Alexander spoke again. 'And she only got into the business through her old man.'

Ah, that at least was true. Her father was a popular conjuror called Charles De Vere (at least, he was called that by the time he lived in Paris and opened a magic shop). His wife performed magic too, in the Chinese style. So yes, Ionia – originally named Clementine – did have a head start in the business.

'But she built it up herself,' I protested, 'and she was very popular.'

'Popular!' snorted Lafayette. 'She just gave the public a lot of fluff, fancy pictures. No real, hard stuff that takes years of practice – no knuckle-busting sleight of hand! She just wafted around the stage waving coloured handkerchiefs! Women shouldn't do magic. Ionia should stick to . . . the Ion-ing!' He laughed in a snorty sort of way at his own joke, and started to speak again. 'She was . . . she was . . .'

Then I heard something in the air. A faint jangling sound. I scanned the posters round the room. All the magicians had suddenly frozen, their eyes looking beyond me. Except for Lafayette, who was still stuttering mid-sentence and was now looking very uncomfortable. He huffed a bit and his lips pursed together very tightly.

The back of my neck started to prickle. Feeling very apprehensive, I slowly turned round.

And saw an astonishing vision!

A tall woman was standing just a few feet away, framed by the little alcove, her arms raised in a dramatic gesture, pointing towards the heavens – it must have been her jangling bangles that I could hear. Her gown was covered with jewels and sequins that reflected the light in the room, sending little rainbow patterns on to the walls and ceiling. She looked every bit like . . . a Greek goddess.

As I gazed at her, she turned her beautiful dark eyes towards me. 'Be'old,' she intoned in a distinct French accent, 'Ionia, ze Goddess of Mystery!' She seemed to be surrounded by a glowing aura – really very magical.

I pulled myself together. How do you greet Ionia, the Goddess of Mystery?

'Welcome to Hackney,' I said rather weakly, feeling that the goddess probably hung out in far more glamorous places as a rule.

Lowering her arms, she put her hands on her hips and looked round the room.

'So you 'ave little respect for ze magic zat women can do,' she said. 'You poor fools! 'Ow little you know. Prepare to be amazed.'

Ionia gestured towards the centre of the room. I turned around and to my surprise a large tent-like structure had materialised there. There were pillars at each corner, holding up flimsy curtains. The opening to the tent was pulled almost completely open so I could see there was nothing inside.

Ionia suddenly clapped her hands together with a sound as sharp as a pistol shot. Another woman came out of the tent, stepping out from behind one of the columns, dressed in a plain white robe. She was holding an old-fashioned butterfly net on a long pole, which she handed to Ionia, then bowed and returned to the tent.

Ionia faced the room, holding the butterfly net if it were a golden sceptre. There wasn't much space for her to swing it, but the cobwebs hadn't been cleaned from the corners of the room for a while so I hoped she might knock some of those out by mistake. 'Regard, gentlemen,' she announced (perhaps she'd overlooked Talma), 'I shall bring to earth ze very birds of ze sky.'

With that, she held the end of the pole and began to sweep it elegantly through the air, as mysterious Egyptian-sounding music started up within the tent. The net was clearly empty. Ionia looked as if she was scanning the air carefully. Suddenly she swooped the net downwards with some force, and I could clearly see something white instantly appear inside it. With a dramatic gesture, Ionia brought the net to ground level, gave it a little shake, and two white doves hopped out. The magician dropped her net, bent to the ground and picked up the birds, one on each hand. They looked absolutely beautiful and not a bit shaken from being produced from nowhere. Ionia bowed deeply to her audience.

Le Roy and Talma were applauding politely, and so was Devant. The other magicians glared out with folded arms.

'Lafayette performed it with so much more style, and it was his routine,' muttered Alexander. I looked around to see Lafayette chewing his upper lip and looking quite annoyed.

I did my bit, clapping enthusiastically and saying, 'Encore!' Nice, and elegantly done, but not a showstopper. Then again, I had been rather spoiled for choice this past year.

Ionia seemed to take no notice of our reaction, but placed the birds on a little Egyptian-style perch and clapped her hands again. The noise was beginning to hurt my ears.

The white-robed woman came back out of the tent, this time holding a number of large metal rings. She passed the rings to Ionia, lifted up the little stand with the doves (which had been sitting very still) and returned to the tent.

'And now,' declared Ionia, again to the accompaniment of tinkling music, 'I shall perform with ze ancient Chinese rings.'

A low groan came from the direction of Lafayette.

Undeterred, Ionia proceeded to manipulate the rings, first showing that they were solid, and then twisting and turning them so they seemed to melt into each other. There were six of them all together.

She did this enchantingly well. The metal hoops really did seem to be melting together and apart. It was truly magical. She ended by spreading her two hands wide with a flourish and showed that the six rings which had been separate a few moments before had all now linked together into a long chain. I was truly impressed. I'd tried learning the Chinese Linking Rings a few times and always found them very difficult. Ionia had made them look really beautiful. Le Roy, Talma and Devant were applauding, and even the other magicians were nodding their approval. Though Lafayette had to say, 'Her mother did that first – and she was better.'

Things seemed to be looking up. Once more Ionia did that pistol-shot effect with her hands (made me jump every time – I was now wishing she wouldn't do it quite so much), and the curtains behind her swept open. Inside were two white-robed women, each holding the side of a large, brightly coloured mummy case (rather like mine). A thick cable rose from the top of it into the ceiling of the tent.

Ionia gazed imperiously at her audience. 'And now,' she announced, 'I shall call on ze powers of Ancient Egypt.'

The Goddess of Mystery turned around in a swirl of sparkling gown, strode towards the mummy case and opened the door. A lady wearing a long white robe stepped forward and walked into the case, shutting the door behind her. The case then began to rise into the air, suspended on the wire. Ionia and her remaining assistants pushed the case so it turned round and round. Then they steadied it, and Ionia opened the door. 'Be'old,' she said, 'ze servant of Isis is still present.' Sure enough, we could see the white-robed figure inside.

Ionia closed the door and, taking a step back, clapped her hands sharply (that noise again!). The mummy case flew open – to reveal an empty interior. Ionia turned round and looked at the far end of the room, calling, 'Come forward, servant of Isis!'

We all looked around, and by the far wall stood the white-robed woman, bowing. She straightened up and walked towards Ionia, while the Egyptian music played again.

There was some clapping from her audience, mostly from Le Roy, Talma, Devant and me – but also mutters of 'Saw that coming a mile off' and 'It's just a poor imitation of your "Flying Visit" illusion, isn't it, Le Roy?' from the more grumpy old magicians.

The assistant reached the tent and stood with the other white-robed woman by the empty mummy case. Ionia stood facing us all, her head lifted high.

'Hah!' she exclaimed. 'You do not appreciate ze artistry of Ionia – ze Goddess of Mystery! I shall show you a wonder of such magnitude that you will be mystified for ever more!'

With that, she quickly pulled the curtains shut all round the tent, and with a final flourish of her arm that made her bangles jangle, slipped inside.

For a couple of seconds there was only the distant sound of a mysterious instrument, which sounded a bit like a violin. Then suddenly there was that familiar CRACK! of a handclap (I jumped yet again) and the curtains enclosing the tent flew open.

We'd seen the tent just moments before, and it was empty apart from the assistants and the mummy case. What we saw took our breath away. It wasn't possible! It was now transformed. We saw before us a walled oriental garden, with the domes of a palace in the background. Ornate columns and decorative screens framed the scene, while colourful flowers spilled from elegant pots. Fountains spouted water in graceful cascades and braziers blazed with bright fire. Doves were flying overhead and one of the white-robed assistants seemed to be floating in mid-air – another was standing on a platform, like a trapeze, again in mid-air. The mummy case, suspended from its cable, was spinning impossibly fast and two tall men wearing striped robes and carrying spears stood guard at either side of the stage. Even the plain floor of the tent was transformed – it was now covered with tiles in mystical-looking patterns, while at the front, five jewel-like tiles spelt out the name *IONIA* in elaborate capitals.

The goddess herself had been transformed and was wearing a totally different gown, gold this time, studded with bright sequins and beads. A jewelled tiara on her head, she stood upright, gazing proudly at us – then swept into a low bow, stretching out her arms either side of her.

We were stunned. For a moment nobody made a sound. And then – a thunder of applause and shouts of 'Bravo! Bravo!' Everyone was clapping madly, even the grumpy old-school magicians – they knew a classy act when they saw one. No rude comments about female magicians now! This was a

truly astonishing finale.

Ionia graciously acknowledged the applause. When we finally stopped, she clapped once more, and the curtains jerked closed again to enclose the whole tableau, while she remained outside.

She smiled at us, gazing round the room. 'Well, gentlemen –' catching the eye of Talma, she added – 'and Madame, I am glad to see that you can appreciate ze work of ze Goddess of Mystery at last. I shall retire to my tent for a moment to attend to my people. I will then rejoin you.'

With a swish of golden robe and a glitter of sequins, she was gone.

The Divine Miss I

While the magicians were excitedly discussing that final illusion – as spectacular as it was unexpected – I sank down on my sofa. What an experience. What a woman – and what a life she had. In some ways it was as exotic as her act.

She was born in Brussels, in 1888, one of the eight children of Charles De Vere (who was born Herbert Shakespeare Gardiner Williams, no less, in England), and his wife, Julia Ferritt, who performed her magic act under the name Okita. With both parents working as magicians (her dad was known as 'Le Mystificateur Comique'), and living literally above the magic shop in Paris, young Clementine seemed destined to enter the business of enchantment. But first she got married, when she was just sixteen, to a lion-tamer – obviously a girl who liked to live dangerously. She started working professionally around 1910, and in a very short career – which lasted only two or three years – she toured Europe with her

own act, which was very well received.

Some time in 1913, she met a Russian prince called Vladimir Eristavi-Tchitcherine. By now she was divorced from the lion-tamer, and she married the prince.

So she went from goddess to princess – and by all accounts she made the most of being 'royal'. She put her time on the stage behind her and never mentioned it again. Quite a dangerous time to be a princess too – during the Russian Revolution! I'd heard that she'd had to spend three months living in the basement of a hotel in Moscow. She and the prince eventually divorced, but Princess Clementine Eristavi-Tchitcherine kept her title till the end of her life – which was a long one. She died in 1973 and was buried in Paris.

All this was going through my mind while I gazed at the tent that had materialised in my poster room. I wasn't seeing the grand princess, but Ionia in her magical prime.

Suddenly the front curtain shifted and Ionia stepped back into the room, still wearing the golden gown studded with sequins. Some of these had become loose and were dropping off on to the floor. It was as if she left a sparkling trail behind her.

I stood up as she came towards me, holding out her hand. I didn't know if I was expected to kiss it (this is the twenty-first century – no one does that any more!), so I shook it quickly, saying, 'Thank you, La Belle Ionia –' I knew that was another of her titles – 'for a truly wonderful performance.'

It was the right thing to say, anyway. She nodded

graciously, and said, 'Let us sit down.'

She was obviously relaxing now. She glanced round the room and smiled. 'I see zat I have shut them up!'

As she was in a good mood, I decided to ask her straight out. 'Could you possibly show me another of your marvellous illusions, something that I might be able to learn?'

She smiled again. 'But, of course,' she said graciously. 'Zat is what I am 'ere for. I have one zat is very good to do at 'ome – as long as you 'ave a good cleaner!'

A Magical Snowstorm

By now, Ionia's assistant – the ex-servant of Isis – was sitting tidily on the floor in front of the curtained tent, which was pulled shut again. Ionia turned to her and said, 'Will you bring to me two sheets of ze tissue paper, ze little glass bowl and my mama's Chinese fan.'

Her assistant nipped behind the curtain and quickly came back with the paper, the bowl and the fan, all resting on a little Egyptian-style table.

She put the paper and the fan on my coffee table, and stood

holding the bowl.

Ionia now asked me, 'Monsieur, would you be so kind as to tell my assistant where she may fill ze bowl with water?'

I wondered why Ionia didn't just use one of the fountains she had just mysteriously produced, but didn't want to seem rude. I politely pointed the assistant in the direction of the kitchen. I wished I'd done the washing-up from the day before, but it's not one of my favourite chores (not that I have *any* favourite chores). I also hoped she would be able to use my rather strange modern taps that looked like something off the Starship Enterprise. But before I knew it I could hear the sound of the tap running and a few moments later in she came, holding the bowl filled with water.

Ionia now stood up and began tearing the paper into little pieces, dropping them into the bowl. When all the paper was soaked, she pulled all the bits out with her elegant fingers and squeezed it in one fist, delicate drops of water falling back into the bowl. She then reached out to the coffee table with her other hand and shook the fan open. She began to wave it gently over the damp tissue in her other hand. Nothing happened for a moment, and the room was dead quiet.

Then, slowly, small pieces of dry paper started to flutter into the air, just like butterflies. The more she fanned, the more paper fluttered out of her hand, until a whole blizzard of confetti-like paper was swirling around the room. As it settled, we all applauded vigorously, Ionia bowing once more. I had seen this now famous magical effect performed on

television, but never in my own home! I didn't look forward to hoovering up the pieces, but that was a small price to pay. I could see what she meant by a cleaner – she probably had a few servants as a princess, but I only had a vacuum cleaner!

After the applause died down and Ionia had taken her final bow, she walked over to me. 'And now, Monsieur, for ze secret lesson!'

She clicked her fingers (a relief from the pistol-shot hand-clapping!) and a second assistant stepped out of the tent, carrying something that looked like a tube.

Ionia took it from her and handed it to me. I could see now that it was a roll of paper – a scroll, like they used to have in the (very) old days before books were invented. A red ribbon was tied round it.

"Ere you are, Monsieur,' said Ionia. 'I 'ope it will 'elp you in your magique. My papa translated it into English especially for you.'

'Th-thank you,' I stammered, and she bestowed another of her dazzling smiles on me.

'When you read it, remember me,' she said. As if I'd forget!

The curtain of the tent had been swept open – I just caught a glimpse of the amazing display inside. Ionia stepped through, followed by her assistant. And then I heard a voice behind me whispering, 'Ionia – Ionia – Goddess of Mysss-tery!' I turned round – but was wary of missing her as she disappeared. By now I had learned all about misdirection!

I turned back round and the tent was still there. Now the voice seemed to be coming from inside it. I stepped closer and closer but the tent seemed to be very still, with a mysterious glow coming from it. I wondered what would happen if I peeked inside. I lifted my hand up towards the tent and suddenly felt quite nervous. *Oh, get a grip!* I told myself.

And as I touched the tent the weirdest thing happened. It seemed to completely collapse. Not in a violent way – it just deflated and shrank, as if it was a giant balloon with the plug pulled out of it. I kept hold of the curtain with one hand as the tent shape vanished completely. The pictures on the walls vibrated slightly from the circulating air. And all of a sudden I was left holding the tent cloth loosely in my hand. The rest of the room looked entirely normal.

I heard one more whisper of the word 'Ionia'. It was coming from behind me, where her poster was, so I spun around, dropping the cloth on the floor. Ionia was back hanging on the wall, as beautifully but inanimately as she had done for years.

Then I realised I was still holding her scroll in my other hand. I carefully undid the ribbon and unrolled the paper. There was a heading in big letters at the top – *An Ionian Snowstorm* – then some little pictures and quite a lot of writing. It was indeed how to perform the magic she'd just shown me – fantastic!

I carefully rolled up the scroll again, tying it with the ribbon and placing it safely on my table. I was dying to try out the snowstorm illusion: it was a beautiful piece of magic. It'd take a fair bit of preparation, but that's the thing about the world of illusion. You might spend a lot of time and care to get ready for a piece of magic which is over in five seconds! But your audience will probably remember it for years. I would certainly remember Ionia's performance for as long as I lived.

An Ionian Snowstorm

You Will Need

Tissue paper – 2 large white sheets, 10 multicoloured sheets
(Make sure you use thin tissue paper, not crêpe.)
A hollow egg
(The easiest way to do this is to hard boil an egg for breakfast and make the smallest hole you can get away with at the top – just the size of a small teaspoon – and eat the contents of

the egg very carefully! Try to scoop out all the egg and then carefully rinse the inside with water. You can also take out the insides of a raw egg if you are careful by making a hole at one end, breaking up the yolk with the flat end of a tea-spoon and tipping it out. Either way ask a grown-up to help you.)

A hat or shoebox

A glass bowl

A Chinese fan

(If you can't get hold of a Chinese fan, any style will do as long as you can create a good breeze with it!)

<u>To Prepare</u>

You will use the two white sheets of tissue paper in your per-formance, so put these to one side. Cut up the other sheets into many little pieces – I shall call these 'confetti'. You can cut the tissue paper a few sheets at a time but make sure you break the pieces up so that they don't stick together in clumps. Cut the paper over a shoe box to catch the pieces.

(Be careful with the scissors! As the tissue is so thin, you could probably cut a few thicknesses at once.)

Now pack the confetti into the hollow egg a little at a

time. Be very careful not to break the shell. Push in as much as you can. Place the egg upright into your hat or shoebox (stand it in a little egg cup to prevent it from falling over), and place the fan next to it. You are now ready.

The Performance

Take the two remaining sheets of paper, show them to the audience on both sides, tear them up and drop them into the bowl of water.

Remove the soggy paper from the bowl with your fingers. Squeeze it into a little ball, allowing some of the excess water to drop out. This will make the pieces stick together into a bundle.

Place the soggy pieces on the table in front of you. Explain to your audience you will try to dry them instantly with your magical fan.

With your left hand, reach into the shoebox or hat for the fan. In fact you secretly pick up the egg first in your palm, and then take hold of the fan with your fingertips.

(This is when you 'palm' the egg, holding it so the audience can't see it. Try to keep your hand holding the egg relaxed – and don't look at it!)

The next moves happen quite quickly. Transfer the fan into your right hand, but leave the egg behind in your left hand. As soon as you have passed the fan across, pick up the soggy ball of tissue paper in the same hand as the egg, using the tips of your thumb and forefinger, and squeeze your hand closed around it. This will, of course, crush the egg.

(So your hand will now be full of dry bits of tissue paper falling out of the crushed egg – along with the soggy bits of course!)

Hold your left hand tightly closed around the confetti and broken egg and lift it high in the air. Start to wave the fan quickly underneath with your right hand. When you can feel a good breeze, start to release the pieces of paper. You'll need to keep crushing and moving the broken egg shell in your hand to make all the confetti come out. Try to do this gradually at first, then allow more and more to be released from your hand. They will catch the air currents and fly upwards. If you keep the fan moving quickly you can keep most of the pieces airborne all at once and they will go very high! A guaranteed applause-getter!!

When you have released all the pieces, you will still have the soggy paper in your left hand. Simply close the fan and pass it into your left hand, and put it back into the hat or shoebox together, secretly, with the ball of soggy tissue.

(Take a dramatic bow and enjoy your applause!)

Chapter 9

The Handcuff King

I T WAS NEARLY A YEAR to the day that my magical visitations had begun. A wonderful year of wizardry! Alexander, The Great Lafayette, Le Roy (with Talma and Bosco), Robert-Houdin, Devant, Chung Ling Soo and Ionia – some of the greatest performers from the golden age of magic – had shown me their stunning performances and shared some of their secrets.

That should have been enough for anyone, and yet . . . all along I was hoping that one person in particular would show up. Harry Houdini. The most famous magician of them all – although he became best known for his impossible escapes. He was a living legend and even today, more than eighty years after his death, he's a household name. People still say, 'You'd need to be a Houdini to get out of that . . .'

But he'd never appeared.

Was it because I didn't have a great big colourful poster of him? After all, that seemed to be the way into my house for my magical visitors. On the other hand, Professor Hoffmann had materialised out of his books.

I just had that little publicity picture of Houdini hanging in the hall, advertising a book he wrote back in 1908. It's not anything like my other posters. There's some lettering which proclaims him as 'The World-Famous Jail Breaker and Handcuff King'. And in the middle is a nice black and white photo showing the master magician looking studious, dressed in a slick suit and a bow tie, leaning on the back of a chair. He's clutching a copy of the book – *The Unmasking of Robert-Houdin*.

Magician among the Spirits

Remember my elegant French visitor? As a child, Houdini had been greatly inspired by the great Frenchman's books, and had even chosen his stage name in Houdin's honour. (He thought that 'Houdini' meant 'like Houdin' – hmm, my French isn't that good, so I'm not sure if he was right.) Of course, Houdini never met the man he took his name from, but when he was working in France he travelled to the city of Blois in the hope of introducing himself to Houdin's surviving daughter-in-law. He was expecting to be welcomed with the purest patisserie and the finest fromage. In fact she had no interest in seeing him – Houdin's family were not happy that the brash 'American' (as he claimed to be) had taken the elegant Frenchman's name! They refused to meet him or even give him permission to lay a wreath at his hero's grave.

Houdini was furious. In a bitter temper, he wrote the book that ripped the reputation of his idol to shreds. He claimed that Robert-Houdin was not a great magician, had copied his tricks off earlier magicians and that he was not as much of a success as he had made out in his own writing. Of course, this was nearly all complete twaddle, and Houdini knew it himself – he even went to the trouble of hiding posters in his personal collection which would have clearly shown that he was making false accusations!

Not a man to upset! But that was Houdini all over – no one was going to snub him and get away with it. His huge success and fame were more than matched by his ego!

And, by the way, he was born Erich Weisz, the son of an Orthodox Jewish rabbi, in 1874. And while we think of him now as the typical all-American showman, fizzing with energy and brass-faced nerve, in fact he was born in Budapest, Hungary. Houdini himself started up the legend, claiming he was born in Appleton, Wisconsin, but actually his family migrated there when Erich was a little boy.

It didn't take him long to get into showbiz. He joined a circus at the age of ten, performing card tricks and sleight of hand – relatively standard stuff (though probably not bad for a boy of ten!). After that, he hit the vaudeville trail with his brother Theo, performing standard conjuring routines – card-and-handkerchief tricks – though including early on his trademark escapes.

He invented an amazing act called 'Metamorphosis', which combined a dazzling escape with a stunning magic effect. He first performed it with Theo (or 'Dash') and then with his wife, a tiny woman called Bess. In this amazing illusion, still performed today, Houdini was placed in a strong sack, which was securely tied up with tape, then padlocked and roped inside a trunk. Bess would pull together two curtains hanging from a rail surrounding the trunk, poking her head through to look at the audience. 'One, two,' she would say – her head disappearing for a split second. 'Three' would be spoken by Houdini as he instantly popped his head back through the curtain in her place. They had switched places in the blink of an eye. Houdini would throw the curtains open, revealing the trunk, still padlocked and roped. He would then untie the ropes, lift the lid of the trunk and open the sack to reveal Bess in his place.

An astonishing piece of magic, but for quite a while their fortunes didn't improve, and they were stuck performing in the American theatrical equivalent of fleapits.

Houdini was getting frustrated by his lack of success, when in 1899 he earned his big break. A man called Martin Beck, who ran one of the vaudeville circuits (rather like the variety theatres in Britain), asked Houdini why he didn't fully concentrate on his escape routines, which were much more interesting than his magic. In fact Houdini was never a really great magician. His stocky frame and stubby fingers meant that he would never be seen on the same level as more elegant performers of magic, such as his contemporary, Kellar. The brash showmanship of escapes suited him better, as Beck realised.

This inspired Houdini, who rapidly built up a repertoire of

amazing escape routines and worked regularly for Beck, soon becoming a sensation wherever he went. He was a master at self promotion. In order to publicise his show at one of the largest theatres in New York, he was placed in a straitjacket (a strange garment almost like a tight potato sack with a hole for the head, strapped up with buckles – it was impossible to get out of at the best of times), then hung upside down from a skyscraper, hundreds of feet above the streets. In full view of the crowds he would wriggle his way free! Sometimes he would be locked in a trunk and thrown into the icy river! He issued challenges in advance to the biggest companies in the towns he visited to build the strongest safe for him to appear from or the most secure pair of handcuffs.

He created sensations by escaping from prison cells under the watchful eye of the guards – sometimes stripped naked to show he was not concealing any keys! This in itself was unheard of back in the 1910s and 1920s. Houdini was a master at coming up with ideas that would grab attention and get audiences into the theatre – 'The Vanishing Elephant', 'Walking through a Brick Wall', 'The Chinese Water Torture Cell', 'The Death-defying Milk Churn Escape'.

Houdini was not only a star in the country he had grown up in – the US – but internationally. He was particularly popular in England, and during his tours of Europe he appeared more than once at the Hackney Empire.

His career took an unexpected turn when his mother, Cecilia Weisz, died while he was on tour in Europe. He'd been very close to her, and he was absolutely devastated he hadn't said goodbye. In desperation, he contacted local mediums. These are people who claim to be able to receive messages 'from the other side' – that is, from dead people. They hold seances, where people sit in a darkened room round a table, holding hands, and try to summon spirits to pass on messages. Houdini wanted above all to speak to his beloved mother one last time.

It was now that he became bitterly disillusioned (strange for an illusionist!). He realised the mediums couldn't do what they said they could. Some were well meaning, such as the wife of his friend Sir Arthur Conan Doyle (of *Sherlock Holmes* fame). Lady Conan Doyle claimed to have received written messages from Houdini's mother, but they were all in English. Cecilia Weisz spoke and wrote only Yiddish – a cross between Hebrew and German – so Houdini was not impressed.

But at least she wasn't deliberately trying to trick him. Most mediums were criminal confidence-tricksters, preying on those who had lost loved ones, especially during the First World War, when millions of young lives were lost. People desperate to 'make contact' were easy to dupe with strange sounds and sights in a darkened room.

Over a ten-year period, not one supposed medium showed Houdini a single example that he considered genuine. The fraudsters enraged him, and he embarked on a war with the mediums, exposing their methods in great detail during his shows.

The mediums hated Houdini for exposing them, and were soon predicting his death – he was really bad for business. In fact Houdini did indeed die at the relatively young age of fifty-three. He'd been performing in Montreal, Canada, and had not been feeling in good form. His endlessly demanding schedule had worn him out, and he'd also sprained his ankle – not good for a man who spent a lot of his time hanging upside down.

One day, in his dressing room, he was visited by two students. One of them was sketching the famous magician as he lay peacefully on a bed, but the other – well, it was now that a claim Houdini had made years earlier was to cost him his life. He'd boasted that his stomach muscles were so strong that he could withstand the hardest of punches. All of a sudden, this other student stood up and punched Houdini very hard repeatedly in his stomach. Houdini had not had a chance to tense his muscles and prepare, and unknown to him he had been suffering from appendicitis.

The next day, Houdini and his company travelled to Detroit, where he struggled through what was to be his final performance, on 24 October. He was suffering from a terrible fever. After the show he was rushed into hospital and the next day he was operated on – the surgeons discovered that the punches had ruptured his appendix and the poisons had gone into his bloodstream. In the days before antibiotics the doctors could do very little for him, and Houdini lost his battle for life on Hallowe'en – 31 October 1926. Ever since, a seance has been held on the anniversary of his death to try to contact his spirit – though considering what Houdini thought of mediums, it's lucky for them he's never appeared!

❋

If anybody could be called larger than life, it was Harry Houdini. Every time I passed the little poster of him in my hall, I wished he'd show up. I tried talking to him – 'Harry,' I'd say (in my mind we were good mates), 'you should have seen your old friend Lafayette yesterday – fantastic!' Or: 'Devant showed up this morning – what a show!' Perhaps I was hoping his competitive spirit would rise to the challenge. But nothing – not even the slightest shake of a handcuff or the rattle of a chain . . .

I should do the lottery, I thought – *if I won, then at last I could buy one of his original posters, one that trumpeted 'The greatest sensational mystery ever attempted in this or any other age!' or 'The world famous self-liberator!'* (Houdini never did things by halves! He was very fond of exclamation marks!!!) If I had a poster of him in my collection, perhaps he too would step down from it . . .

Then one day I had a brainwave. Almost a year before, Professor Hoffmann had said I could call on him – and I never had done so. Now I stood in front of my bookshelves and called out to him. 'Hello, professor! Can you hear me?' For a while nothing happened. *He's probably busy doing his home gymnastics*, I thought.

And then, just as I was giving up all hope, with a sudden *POP!* a little dust cloud formed, which instantly turned into the professor – pedalling out of the bookcase on his old-fashioned tricycle!

Quickly applying his brakes, the professor called out, 'Hello again, young man. Well, I must say you've certainly been having a busy time. Fascinating! I wish I'd seen these fellows in action before I wrote my magic books.' He glanced at the posters round the room. 'I do believe I'll have to revise them now!'

He beamed at me through his bushy white beard, while his

eyes twinkled behind his glasses.

'Now tell me,' he went on. 'What can I do for you? A handy tricycling tip, perhaps?'

'Well,' I began. I looked at the posters, and they seemed to be asleep. I still spoke in a whisper, though – I didn't want them hearing me.

'I was wondering,' I said, 'if Houdini was going to appear. I know I haven't got a poster of him, just that little advert in the hall, but I really would love to see him.'

'Hmmm,' said the professor, rocking on his toes. 'I know what you mean. A most remarkable figure in the history of magic. However, Alexander has been taking care of all the arrangements, I believe. Perhaps he has decided not to communicate with him. These American chaps, you know, very competitive.'

Houdini wasn't really American, I thought to myself, but I didn't want to sound like a smart Alec, not to the professor.

I must have looked disappointed, as he added, 'But I'll see what I can do. Now, I must be going – things to do, you know. I think I may have a puncture – or rather my tricycle has.'

With that, he started pedalling again and disappeared in a *POP!* of dust.

As I left the room, I heard a loud sniff coming from Alexander's poster. 'Not enough for you, huh?' came his sarcastic voice. 'Some people are never satisfied.'

I might have known, though, that Houdini, master escapologist, would choose his own way of making an entrance . . .

It was a Friday in April. I'd finally cleared up the last of Ionia's sequins (she seemed to have shed rather a lot for a Goddess of Mystery). I found them in the oddest of places, like between my toes and under the cushions on the sofa. I had my big variety show appearance coming up pretty soon and although I was still waiting to get my confirmed date from the agency I didn't want to be caught unprepared. So most of the evening I'd spent rehearsing my act, working very late trying to perfect a tricky bit of sleight of hand involving a lemon and an ostrich feather. I'd got tired around midnight and had reset the whole show on my prop table in order to carry on practising the following day. Everything was there – the little table with its special holders and secret pockets. I even had my new suit hanging up on the back of the chair. That way, everything was ready for a full dress rehearsal next morning.

When I woke up, the sun was peeping through a little gap

in my curtains. *Going to be a nice day*, I thought. Still feeling drowsy, I was thinking of getting up and making a nice cuppa before practising my act. Everything was blissfully peaceful.

Then suddenly it was as if someone was blowing the loudest trumpet in the world! The noise was coming through the window, splitting the air and hurting my ears. What on earth was going on in my back garden?

It sounded like – no, it couldn't – surely not. It sounded like . . . an elephant! An elephant trumpeting very, very loudly.

Well, it certainly worked more effectively than my alarm clock. Now wide awake, I jumped out of bed and cautiously edged up to the window, my heart thumping.

I grabbed the sides of the curtains and pulled them further apart. I hardly dared to look.

Another blast on the trumpet – no mistaking it now. I stepped back in shock. 'Oh, come on,' I said to myself. 'You know what's out there.' And I did.

There it was, a beautiful full-grown elephant in my back garden, dwarfing the small man standing beside her – the unmistakable figure of Harry Houdini. Here he was at last. I didn't know what had made him appear – did the professor have a quiet word? Did his old friend Lafayette say something to Alexander? Just now, I didn't care.

In the middle of the garden was a huge box, almost the size of a small garage. It had two large doors at the front, which were open to show a double door at the back which two

assistants were in the process of opening. A number of other assistants dressed in black suits stood around the box, which was raised off the ground with large painted wheels. It could only be one thing. 'The Vanishing Elephant!' It was one of Houdini's most celebrated illusions – and the secret had been lost for over seventy years. I couldn't wait!

My neighbours didn't seem to be sharing my enthusiasm. They were peering out of their upstairs windows, their mouths hanging open, goggling. Some of them, still in pyjamas, had obviously only just woken up, like me, and were rubbing their eyes in disbelief. A couple in next-door's garden were standing on tiptoe, trying to look over the wall. Once they saw the giant animal they hurried away and stood by the safety of their back door.

Houdini looked around the collection of faces peering in his direction. He glanced up at my window– I think he saw me peeping through the gap in the curtain, as he gave a quick wink before turning round again.

'Lay-deez and gen-tel-men,' he proclaimed dramatically. 'I ap-pre-ci-ate your full atten-tion!'

Such a performer, I thought. *He probably does a ten-minute spot when he opens the fridge door and the light comes on.*

'Here I have Jen-ny. She weighs ten thou-sand pounds!'

Now I knew that was a lot – about five tonnes by my reckoning – quite a bit heavier than a big car. I tried not to think of what damage Jenny the elephant could do in my back garden. *Bring back Ionia and her sequins*, I thought. *All is forgiven.*

Houdini was talking in a very deliberate way, emphasising e-ve-ry syllable of e-ve-ry word. Not surprising really — he originally presented his vanishing elephant in the Hippodrome in New York, one of the largest theatres ever built (it held over 5,000 people). It reminded me I had heard his voice once before. The Magic Circle Museum in London had a muffled recording of it.

The elephant was standing there, looking very serene with a blue ribbon around her neck and a large wristwatch attached to her leg, although I couldn't really see why she would need to know the time.

Houdini was bellowing again. 'I will place Jen-ny the ten-thou-sand-pound el-e-phant in-to this box. She will dis-ap-pear in two se-conds flat!'

That's what she needs the watch for, I thought, *so she doesn't take too long.*

'Jen-ny, come this way!'

But she wasn't going anywhere. A couple of assistants tried to coax the huge animal towards them with carrots. She gently turned her great grey eyes towards them with a puzzled expression on her face.

Jenny swayed her trunk from side to side and lifted it up in a huge arc. Then suddenly she swung around, her giant feet pounding the grass and making the house shake. Not being familiar with the layout of the average Hackney garden, she caught the side of her body on the brick wall with quite a force. I knew the wall wasn't the strongest thing in the world, and a five-tonne elephant bashing into it was all it needed! It started to collapse into next-door's garden. The neighbours, now huddled together, screamed in terror. *Whoops – I think I'll have a bit of explaining to do when this is all over*, I thought, *not to mention a bill for a new brick wall.*

'You're nothing but a menace!' yelled one neighbour. 'This is Hackney, not a circus! I'm getting on to the council!'

Of course, my neighbours had no idea who they were really watching – I'd explained the strange events of the last few months by saying that I was playing host to a few visiting magicians from around the world (which was sort of true!).

Jenny the elephant hardly noticed the wall. She was now being led by one of the assistants up a small ramp into the front of the box. Houdini had spotted the collapsing wall out of the corner of his eye, but, like the old pro he was, he just carried on as if nothing had happened.

As soon as Jenny was inside the box, two of the other helpers ran to the back and shut the big doors. I could still see Jenny's tail waving out of the front of the garage-sized container.

'Now you see her . . .' yelled the magician – at which the huge front doors were pushed closed. Almost instantly the assistants pulled all the doors open again, front and back. Jenny seemed to have completely vanished. I could see right through to the trees behind.

'And now you don't!' announced The Great Houdini triumphantly.

I was greatly impressed by Jenny's time keeping — it really did seem to have happened in no more than two seconds — but completely astounded, too, that she had just vanished in my back garden! Various neighbours were clapping and whooping and whistling from their windows. Houdini stood bowing deeply, looking very pleased with himself. Through the gap where the collapsed wall had once stood I could see the other neighbours looking very relieved that the elephant had vanished. *At least they got a good view of the performance without a brick wall in the way*, I thought to myself.

'I thank you, lay-deez and gen-tel-men!' Houdini had finished his act. He bowed and then and headed straight towards my back door. Still only wearing my pyjamas, I grabbed a bathrobe and ran down the stairs. The Great Houdini had finally showed up and he'd done it in style!

I ran to my back door, fumbling around with the keys. The top lock was always sticky.

'Can I help you?' a loud American voice said behind me. 'I know a thing or two about locks.'

There stood The Great Houdini himself! He was somehow already inside. I should have known he wouldn't have needed a key to get in.

I was pretty nervous. There was so much I wanted to ask him!

He was looking round the room. 'Ha — I like your posters,' he drawled. 'Except this one here,' he added, pointing, predictably, at Houdin. I could swear Houdin was scowling at him.

'I knew a few of these guys, you know,' he went on. 'And that little old prof tells me they've been doing their stuff here.'

Ah, so that's how he knew. I nodded, still lost for words.

'But you do realise that I – The Great Houdini – am the greatest of them all, don'tcha?'

With that he rolled up his sleeves and began to pull cards out of the air. I remembered he had started off with a card manipulation act early in his career.

I applauded politely. 'Amazing,' I said. Then, remembering the title from an old poster in a history book, I added, 'You really are "The King of Cards".' Flattery, I thought, would probably get me everywhere with Harry Houdini.

'Will you – could you – show me one of your legendary escapes, please?' I'd certainly become more confident in asking my magical visitors to show me things. I had a strong suspicion that Houdini would be my last visitor – he was always top of the bill – and I wasn't going to waste a moment.

He snorted. 'Listen, young feller, I spent the last few years of my career tryin' to stop doin' those darn escapes – tryin' to take things a bit easier, doin' big illusions where I only had to point and wave my arms. I'm tired of escapes,' he said in his distinctive New York drawl. 'I've escaped from just about everything in my time. Steel safes, a Siberian prison van, Scotland Yard. I was nailed into a wooden trunk and thrown into the Hudson River, padlocked into a vat of beer (not sure that was a good idea at all), and someone in Boston even locked me into the carcass of a whale!'

A whale? I was just going to ask him how that worked when I noticed he was looking at my untidy shopping from the night before, spread out across the table, carrier bag and all.

'What you gonna do – challenge me to escape from that Tes-go's bag?' The World Famous Self-Liberating Sensation laughed heartily. 'No, young feller,' he said. 'No escapes today – for me anyhow.'

I obviously looked disappointed, but was slightly puzzled as to what he meant.

He stared again at the posters round the wall. 'So you've been getting ideas from these fellers, have you?'

His eyes settled on the poster of Chung Ling Soo. 'Ah – Billy. Now he was a great magician.' Soo's lips may just have curved upwards a little. 'And Sigmond – Lafayette,' Houdini went on, 'he was a great one too. I gave him his dog, you know.'

'I know,' I said. On Lafayette's poster, the little dog was wagging her tail, and her master didn't look as miserable as usual.

'Well, I'll be darned,' drawled Houdini. 'They ain't gonna outdo me. If these fellers taught you something –' he looked at me with a twinkle in his eye – 'then I'm gonna teach you something you'll never forget!'

✳

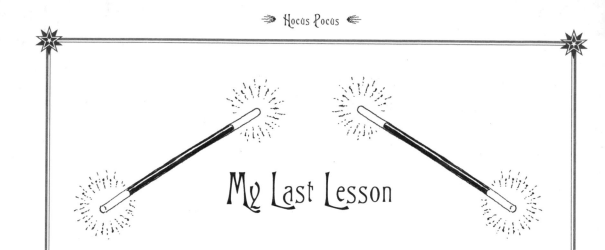

My Last Lesson

He suddenly grabbed my arm and pulled me quite aggressively in the direction of his advertising poster in the hall. Houdini may have been small but he was very strong.

'You know,' he said, not missing a step, 'I'm good at escapin' things – being in one place one moment and some place else another moment . . .'

And with that he swung me towards the picture frame.

At first I felt just the wall, and then a weird tingling sensation all over my body. Images whizzed around in my head – all the master magicians I'd met over the past year, everything they'd taught me, seemed to pass through my eyes in a colourful kaleidoscope.

And suddenly I wasn't in my house any more.

I was standing on a wooden floor and in front of me were dazzling lights. I could hear people walking around and the muffled sound of live music – an upbeat tune I didn't recognise. All around me were giant boxes and machinery and lots of assistants busily pushing them into place. They all seemed to be in quite a hurry.

I was obviously in a theatre. I looked up above me and could see ropes and pulleys, with large cloths and pieces of scenery hanging in the air from wooden bars. I cautiously peered around the curtain in front of me and then it became clear: I was standing at the side of the Hackney Empire stage. But it wasn't quite the theatre I recognised – it looked like the old pictures I'd seen of it from decades ago, like I'd seen it through the opening of Servais Le Roy's poster when I'd watched his amazing 'Asrah' levitation. But this time I was the one on stage peering back out over the audience. Houdini was nowhere to be seen.

I looked through the smoky theatre and could see hundreds – thousands – of people, four levels of them: the theatre was packed! Men in dark suits, women in long skirts, some of them wearing big hats (*Too bad if you're sitting behind them*, I thought). They were pushing past each other to get into their seats. I looked through the narrow gap in the curtain to see where the music was coming from. There was an orchestra of about fifteen musicians all playing away, with a smartly dressed conductor. There was a buzz of excitement in the auditorium – it seemed to be the start of a performance.

Above the sides of the stage, just below the exotic Moroccan balconies, were two large slotted frames. I knew these were used for displaying the name of the next act that would be appearing onstage. I could see a small, bearded man dressed in shirtsleeves behind it. He had a pile of large cards in his hand, all with different names on, but I couldn't see any of them clearly. He was quickly sorting through them. He found one and leaned forward, about to slot it into the open frame. *Who can it be?* I wondered. Who was I going to see perform?

And then I noticed I wasn't dressed in my pyjamas any more. It was impossible: somehow I was in my suit – the one I'd set up the night before. I felt the side of my pockets – they seemed to have props set up in them. And what I saw made me petrified. As I felt my pockets I bumped into something behind me. I looked back at what it was and a feeling of panic and dread washed over me.

It was the table for my own act, all set up and ready to go. *Surely not*, I thought to myself. *It can't be.* I peered back through the curtain to see which name had appeared in the display at the side of the stage. It simply said: *Special Guest.* I wondered what this lesson might be. Surely I couldn't be going out onstage for an audience waiting to see Houdini?

And then it dawned on me . . . the mysterious letter, the booking for the London Theatre – this was it! Could it have been that Houdini was involved all along, and this was my big test – my final lesson? Perhaps he'd got me to prepare for it before showing up?

I looked across the stage. A man with a curly moustache and long tail coat was standing in a spotlight in the centre.

'And for our first act this evening,' the man announced, 'we have a special guest. He's a local lad, wants to become a great magician. He's worked hard on his show and he's gonna perform it for you tonight. Ladies and gentlemen, please give a big round of applause to – our mystery guest!'

As he was speaking, I felt blind panic. Had I set up the act properly the night before? What would the rowdy Hackney Empire crowd think of it? I felt sick at the thought.

But I had no time to waste. A glamorous showgirl dressed in a glittering sequinned outfit with a number of feathers sticking out of her hair had grabbed my table of magic props and placed it into the centre of the stage. My music, which I was so familiar with hearing on CD, was being played by the orchestra. They were hitting all the right notes – but it did sound very unfamiliar being played live. I stood frozen to the spot. The last time I felt this afraid about stepping on the stage I'd got so nervous that I had dropped my magic wand into the orchestra pit, never to be retrieved.

Next to me was a man in a dark suit. 'It's you, son – you're on.' He gave me a little shove.

I stepped on to the stage and the audience didn't seem that pleased to see me. There were a few handclaps, and some whistles – but also some jeers. I was not going to have an easy time.

Forcing myself to bow and smile, I reached into my pocket, my hands trembling, to grab a silk handkerchief – not even being sure it would be there. But it was – I ran it through my fingers, performed the necessary sleight of hand and *pop!* – it changed into a stick. I put it to the side of the table. Reaching up to my lapel, I removed another silk handkerchief and showed it on both sides. I tied it into a knot and placed the knot in my mouth. I lifted it up to produce two fluttering doves – this was met with a smattering of polite applause. But there were still lots of people just talking among themselves and not paying much attention at all. *This'll get them*, I thought.

I clicked my fingers in the air and a flash of fire erupted from them (good trick that one – I'd used it since taking part in Young Magician of the Year!). A few more of them shut up. I picked up my magic stick – *whoosh* – another dove fluttered on top of it.

But the audience now seemed to be getting restless. It was no good. My act was just not polished enough to impress this audience, or perhaps I just didn't have the experience to pull it off. They'd probably seen Chung Ling Soo, Lafayette, Devant – all of them – this year. And here I was with my pathetic dove act. I was dying a death. As I whisked the cloth away from my dove cage to reveal a rabbit, the audience greeted me with indifferent applause. The act hadn't gone at all well.

I began to walk into the wings, when the compère grabbed my arm.

'An interesting taster of beginner's magic,' he announced to the audience. 'But for his finale tonight this brave young man will be placed into a milk churn full of water with its lid padlocked and chained on to the top. It will be impossible for him to obtain air in this position. He'll have no longer than four minutes to escape – or he'll meet death by drowning.'

There was a stir of interest in the audience, but I was speechless. The back curtain had opened to reveal what looked like four tall clothes rails pushed together in a square, quite a bit taller than me. It looked like the sort of place you might try on clothes in a shop – but I knew that's not what I was going to be doing. There were long curtains hanging on all sides – the front one was pulled open to reveal a large aluminium milk churn standing inside, filled to the brim with water. Before I knew it, two burly assistants had taken me by either arm and were leading me towards the churn. I was completely terrified and instinctively started struggling to get away. My biggest dream was rapidly turning to a terrifying nightmare. One of the assistants whispered to me, 'Don't worry, Harry will help you out – take a deep breath!'

Now I was being forced into the water tank. I took the biggest deep breath I could possibly manage. My life was now in the hands of a master magician!

One of the assistants pushed my head down below water

level. As I felt the cold water touch my face I could already feel my lungs, full of air, pressing inside me. Now the lid was being placed on top. It had gone pitch black. I could hear the sounds of chain scraping against the metal sides of the milk churn, and then the clicking sounds of locks being snapped shut.

Four minutes! I might just be able to hold my breath for forty seconds, tops. But four minutes? I'd be drowned, no doubt about it. As I heard the muffled sound of the curtain being drawn closed in front of me I felt completely panicked, desperately trying to hold my breath, and my lungs were already getting tired. Maybe this was it – my final lesson – but surely not drowning on the stage of the Hackney Empire at the time of Houdini? That couldn't happen. I hadn't even been born yet!

As my lungs began to feel as if they were about to burst, I heard a thud on the top of the can. And then a sliding sound. Within seconds the pitch blackness had transformed into light – the lid of the milk can had been opened. Instinctively I pushed my feet against the bottom of the can, forcing my head out of the water to gasp for air. And there, through my streaming eyes, I could see the blurry vision of Harry Houdini, holding a key in one hand and four padlocks in the other. He had unlocked the milk churn and released me.

'Get outta there before you drown, young feller!' he whispered to me.

I looked up and gasped – this was stranger than I ever could have imagined.

'How – how did you get here?' I spluttered, coughing water out of my mouth.

'Not so loud,' Houdini hissed. 'We don't wanna make too much noise.' I could hear the orchestra playing a dramatic tune on the other side of the curtain. Houdini pointed down to an open trapdoor – he'd secretly let himself up inside the curtain from under the stage to release me.

'Now I didn't get help like this when I started out, young feller,' he muttered, 'but you know I said I'd teach you the biggest lesson of all? Well, that was standin' on the stage of this great theatre and playin' to a real audience. You can practise all you like, but the only thing you get good at by practising is practising.'

He went on. 'And the other lesson is – don't knock us old guys. We knew what we were doin' – you can learn a lot from us. We were out there doin' it, knocking socks off audiences, long before your parents or even your grandparents were born. Most of you guys now wouldn't stand a chance if you were pitched against us grand masters from the past.'

By now I had got my breath back and had climbed carefully out of the water tank, my suit drenched. As Houdini was talking he had popped the lid back on and was relocking the padlocks around the outside of the tank. He was careful to arrange the chain and locks – I guessed in exactly the way they had been left, so that the audience wouldn't know they had been moved.

I stared at him in astonishment. 'That letter, the agency,

was it you? Is this the show it referred to?'

Houdini smiled broadly. 'Well, young man.' He chuckled. 'When you have a few minutes, try rearranging the letters of the name of the agency! But you'll have time to do that later – one more lesson before I go,' he said. 'When those curtains are opened, the crowd is gonna go mad. You know why? Because you did somethin' that grabbed them. I'm not sayin' you have to cheat death to do that – but just think of all the other guys who you've seen. Lafayette and his storytellin', Devant and his dramas and death rays, Alexander contactin' the spirits and readin' your mind – these are all things that the audience could care about. Make sure that you don't bore them with stuff they don't give a cent about. Oh – and one last thing. When I'm gone, wait here another coupla minutes. They think you'll be a gonner in four, so wait four minutes twenty – then throw the curtain back as if you're within an inch of your life. They'll never know you were ready in under a minute. Keep 'em waitin' – there's no point doin' an escape quickly. Makes it look too easy!'

He grinned widely. 'That's showmanship, my friend, and I should know. Don't forget the power of stillness, stoppin' – most magicians today just rush through everything. You think I got where I did by rushin'? Here, read this while you're waitin'. See you around, feller.'

And with that he thrust a newspaper into my hand and, before I could say anything back to him, the great escapologist had slipped back through the trapdoor and disappeared. I looked down: *The Hackney and Kingsland Gazette*, dated 4 February 1911. I sat on the floor and pondered, my heart still thumping in my chest. Behind the curtain I could hear the crowd chattering, people coughing, muttering to each other in a concerned way. What did Houdini mean about the name of the agency – Around Eightieth? I started to think about the letters. H-o-u-d-i-n-i , of course! They were all in there – and T-h-e-G-r-e-a-t – that's what it spelled out. The letter *had* been from him and the clue was there all the time!

'Three minutes and forty-five seconds,' I heard the compère announce.

The audience started to go wild, a lady screaming, 'Let the man out!' Was Houdini right – could I hold it a few more seconds?

'Four minutes,' the compère announced. Now the crowd really were going crazy. I counted slowly – twenty seconds more – and threw back the curtain, staggering forward and pretended to gasp for breath, The crowd rose to its feet, clapping and cheering, whistling and stamping. As I scanned the audience, taking my bows, I spotted the distinctive figure of Houdini at the back of the auditorium. He tipped his hat to me with a broad smile before slipping through the exit door.

I had gone down a storm, thanks to him.

✳

I don't know how long I stood there, on the stage of the old Hackney Empire, taking bow after bow, the audience's applause ringing in my ears. What I do know is that as the red plush curtains swept in front of me, I straightened up – and was looking at my bedroom curtains, flapping in the breeze from the open window, and was dressed in my pyjamas again!

It took me a while to get my bearings – but yes, that was my back garden, the grass full of ruts from the wagon, the wall half-demolished. It did really happen, Houdini had appeared to me at last. And, typical of the man – he wasn't like my other magical visitors – he didn't show me exactly how to do one of his illusions.

But I learned the biggest lesson of all. I'd had the opportunity to perform in front of an audience who had seen all the greatest magicians who ever lived. And I knew with certainty that he was the last of my magic mentors – who could follow him?!

But that was all a few years ago now and ever since my magical year, I've tried to practise what I learned. I can't play the big theatres and variety bills like the old-timers did – things have changed a lot in the entertainment world – but I still remember the advice I was given: practise till you're perfect, build up the big picture, make the whole performance mysterious and wonderful and unforgettable for the audience. The world is a magical place, and that's the magician's job: to remind people of that fact and to give them a fantastic sense of wonder.

So that's what I've been sharing with you in this story — what magic is all about, why it's fascinated audiences for hundreds if not thousands of years and why it will go on doing so for as long as there are human beings on this planet.

Chapter 10

A Miscellany of Mystery: Magic Inspired by the Masters

My astonishing wizardly visitors inspired me to gather together more magic for you to learn. Whether it's amazing card tricks with Robert-Houdin, or baffling coin magic with Talma and Le Roy, this miscellany of mystery is all connected in some way to my magical guests. Houdini – always the showman – rounds everything off with some challenges for you, and an impressive 'Grand Illusion'. You'll see that some of the tricks are quick and simple, and others are more elaborate performance pieces – but they'll all give you and your audience a lot of enjoyment!

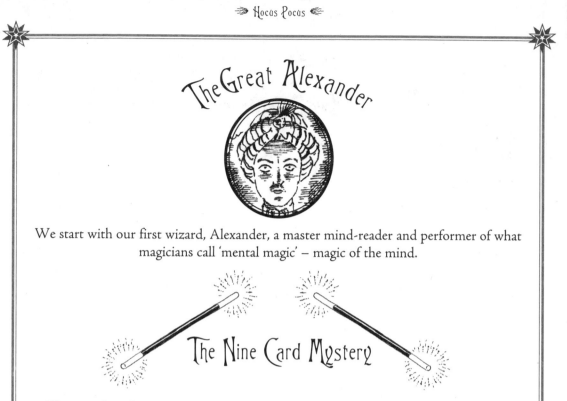

The Great Alexander

The Nine Card Mystery

We start with our first wizard, Alexander, a master mind-reader and performer of what magicians call 'mental magic' – magic of the mind.

This puzzling demonstration relies on a secret code from an accomplice to transmit information. It's perfect for performing in a room at home for a few friends.

The Magic

You leave the room while a friend shuffles a pack of cards and then lays out nine playing cards, face up, in three rows of three. A spectator then selects a card and points to it. When you return to the room you are instantly able to name the chosen card without any apparent clues. This can be repeated several times and becomes increasingly baffling to the audience!

Performance

The person dealing the cards is your secret accomplice, and you have agreed a special code which no one else will be able to detect!

When you re-enter the room, the accomplice simply places their thumb on the back of the remaining pack of cards in a position to indicate where the chosen card is. If their thumb is resting at the centre of the pack, you'll know with the quickest glance that the selected card is located in the centre of the square of nine laid-out cards. Centre left means the card is on the second row (centre) on the left. This works easily and clearly for any of the nine positions. You should always say the name of the card (such as 'two of diamonds') rather than its position.

Every time you repeat the 'mind-reading experiment', get your accomplice to shuffle the old set of nine cards back into the pack and deal out a different set of nine face-up cards. This does not affect the method at all, but makes the demonstration more mysterious to your audience and acts as 'misdirection'. Although, as a rule, it's best not to repeat a trick straight away (your audience are more likely to spot the secret), this demonstration becomes more amazing if it's shown two or three times – but don't overdo it!

Terrific Telepathy

This is guaranteed to baffle your audience – it really seems that you can read someone's mind! The method is almost embarrassingly simple, but it does require some acting on your part . . .

The Magic

After suggesting a general subject – let's say it's sport – you request that the audience give you ten different specific examples. This might turn out to be tennis, football, ping-pong, and so on. You write down the suggested words on separate pieces of paper, fold them up and put them into a hat. A member of the audience randomly picks out one of the pieces, unfolds it without anyone else seeing and concentrates on the word written on it. You dramatically identify the correct word!

Preparation

There's not much to get ready. Just find a small piece of plain paper for each member of the audience (though not more than about ten – otherwise you'll be going on for ages), something to write with, and a hat or bowl to put the folded papers in.

Performance

The secret is that as the audience are suggesting the different words, you actually write the same one again and again – the first word that was called out. Fold up the

papers one by one after you've written on them, and place them into a hat or bowl. As you're rewriting the first word you're given (let's say it's *football*), you have to pretend to be writing the new word. So someone may suggest *motor racing*, and you murmur 'mo-tor ra-cing' as you write *football*!

When you have all the suggestions, mix up the bits of paper and tell your audience you've been working hard on developing your telepathic powers, and you'll prove it. Ask a member of the audience to choose one of the folded pieces, open it up without showing you what it is and concentrate on the word. Then you have a bit more acting – the presentation, remember? 'I see a field, and men running about . . . There's a ball – is it round or oval? . . . It's round . . .' And you announce triumphantly: 'It's football!'

Of course, the subject doesn't have to be sport – it could be plants, sweets and chocolates, pop singers, hobbies, planets – anything that you can divide into a list ('rabbits' wouldn't be a good general topic, but 'animals' would be fine!). One other tip: just make sure nobody gets hold of the other bits of paper, otherwise your reputation as a master mind-reader won't last long.

It's Mentally Mathemagical!

Here's an amazing apparent feat of mind-reading – but the secret is purely mathematical!

The Magic

A spectator chooses a secret number and you ask them to make a series of calculations. You've already predicted the final answer and placed it in an envelope which has been on view from the beginning of the routine – and it turns out to be correct!

Performance

Show the audience a sealed envelope – you explain that it contains a prediction you made earlier. After handing a spectator a notebook and pen, ask them to write down three different numbers from one to nine (excluding zero) in a line without letting you see. Tell them to reverse this three digit number and write it next to the original one.

Then ask them to subtract the smaller number from the larger.

They must then reverse that answer, and add this to the previous total.

Ask them to read the total out loud. Your prediction matches their number perfectly!

Example

Let's say 6, 2 and 9 are the spectator's three chosen numbers – so they'd write them together like this: 629

They'd reverse the number and get 926 . . .

Subtract the smaller number from the larger: 926 – 629 = 297 . . .

And then reverse the number 297 to get 792 . . .

Then they'd add this to the previous total: 297 + 792

That's it!

Why don't you do this yourself now? Get a pen and paper and follow the instructions above – start with three different single-digit numbers. If after doing the first subtraction your number ends up being only two digits, then add a '0' at the beginning (so 99 would become 099 – then you'd reverse it to get 990)

Let's see if my prediction is correct – it's at the bottom of page 293. But don't look at it until you've got to the end of your calculation . . .

Was I correct? In fact, amazingly, this is always the answer – no matter which three-digit number is chosen in the first place. This is an example of mathematical magic that works itself – so you don't need to worry about it going wrong as long as your spectator can add up. (If you want to make extra sure you could give them a calculator to check before revealing your prediction.) You can just get on with making your presentation as exciting as possible!

Reading between the Lines

This is a very interesting trick – it seems to be a demonstration of handwriting analysis. I actually performed this in my first ever magic show!

The Magic

Members of your audience write down a few words on individual pieces of paper, using identical pens. The papers are then shuffled – and you are able to identify who wrote what, just by looking at the handwriting! (And no, you don't already know what their writing looks like!)

Preparation

You need a sheet of paper and a pen for each member taking part – say, six. (The paper and the pens should look identical to the audience.) You will also need some hardback books or clipboards for the audience to rest their paper on as they write. The secret is that although the papers all look the same, you've secretly marked them in the top right-hand corner with tiny pencil marks – very lightly, so that they're invisible unless you know what you're looking for. Simply draw a series of very faint lines in number order – so 1 is I, 2 is II, 3 is III, 4 is IIII and so on. You pile up the papers in order, 1 at the top, down to 6 at the bottom.

Performance

Hand out the secretly marked papers to the spectators from left to right in strict order, then hand them the six pens. Point out to them that the pens must be identical, otherwise you'd know who had written what straight away!

Ask the spectators to scribble a few words down, making sure they don't write anything that would give clues to their identity. Get one of them to collect all the papers and mix them up, so you couldn't possibly know the order. When you're handed the papers, it's a simple matter for you to find the secret mark and therefore locate which spectator wrote the words.

The success of this routine is all in the presentation and acting. You should comment on the handwriting by saying, 'This writing looks like it has a lot of loops in it – so I think the person who wrote it must have curly hair!' Or you could say that the writing is long and thin, so the person must be tall, or that the writing looks as if it's been written by a younger or older person. (You should only make comments which are relevant to the person who has really written the words.)

The more you enchant the audience with your chat about analysing the handwriting, the more amazed they will be!

✳

The Great Lafayette

The Leopard Card

Lafayette was the first magician to use wild animals – so here's a wild piece of magic! You know that leopards never change their spots? Well, here's a card that does.

The Magic

You show the audience a piece of card with spots – a bit like a big domino. As you turn the card around the spots magically appear and disappear in a very bewildering way!

Preparation

Use a piece of white card, about 15 cm by 22 cm. You'll also need seven self-adhesive coloured paper spots about the size of £2 coins (these are sold in sticker sheets, in stationery shops). Stick five spots on one side of the card, and two on the other, following the pattern shown here. (Make sure you don't turn the card upside down when you turn it over to stick the other two spots on.) Now your preparation is complete.

    What happens in performance is that you place your fingers on the cards so that certain spots are secretly covered or uncovered. Because your spectator's brain is familiar with the regular patterns of a domino, it imagines there are spots where your hands are positioned, or imagines that the card is blank when really your hand is covering up a spot!

Performance

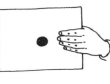

Fig. 1

First, show the side with two spots to the audience, having hidden the outer dot with the fingers of your right hand (fig. 1). The audience will think this card has just one spot.

Next, hold on to the card with your left hand so your fingers are facing you and completely covering the middle spot. Once your hand is in position, turn your left hand so that your fingers are facing the audience. Don't let go with the right hand until you've started to turn the card around, otherwise the audience will see the hidden spot. The audience will imagine the second side has only four spots (fig. 2).

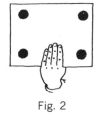

Fig. 2

Next, place your right hand (fingers facing towards you) back on the card, this time covering the space next to the two spots. Once again, turn your hand around so that your fingers now face the audience. (fig. 3). They'll think you've magically changed one spot to three!

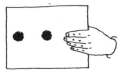

Fig. 3

Finally, place your left hand (fingers towards you) on the card again, this time allowing all five dots to show and covering the gap in the middle. When you turn the card to face the audience, they'll think you've changed four dots to six (fig. 4). Practise in front of a mirror so that you don't accidentally move your hands away too soon. The whole sequence should be smooth, and even the simplest tricks require practice. Your audience will soon have spots before their eyes!

Fig. 4

Sweet Confetti

As we've seen, Lafayette loved to do big showy magic tricks. Here's one that always goes down a treat (probably because there are sweets at the end of it!).

The Magic

The audience see a big bowl filled with confetti on your table. You then show them an empty mug and plunge it right into the bowl, lifting it out full of confetti. You tip the confetti out and do this once or twice more, finally leaving the cup visibly filled to the brim. Then, uttering a magic word, you cover the confetti-filled mug with a handkerchief – whipping it away to reveal that the cup is now amazingly filled with sweets!

Preparation

What You Need

* A large bowl you can't see through (like a coloured plastic basin)
* Two identical mugs
* Loads of confetti. You can make your own by cutting up lots of differently coloured tissue paper and mixing it up thoroughly. You'll need at least half a bowl full – enough to hide one of the mugs under.
* Glue
* Circle of card just a fraction larger than the mouth of the mug
* Blu-tack
* A packet of sweets
* A large scarf or square cloth
* A clear plastic bowl to pour the sweets into at the end

First you have to make a top-secret device which will make the magic happen – a circle of card with confetti stuck on to one surface! Magicians generally call this kind of secret thing a 'feke'. The idea is that when the card is positioned correctly, the mug looks as if it's full to the brim with confetti – but really it's only a thin layer on the very top of the mug.

Place the mug upside down on some card from a cereal packet and draw a line around it with a pencil. Then carefully cut the circular shape out with scissors.

Spread some paper glue or PVA over this circle of card and stick lots of confetti on to it. Once the confetti is properly dry, turn over the disc and place four big blobs of Blu-tack (about the size of garden peas) evenly around the outside edge of the card disc.

Next, place the sweets in the mug, so that it is almost full to the brim – but none of them should stick out above the top. It's best to use sweets that don't rattle noisily against each other, so soft, chewy ones or chocolate-covered goodies are ideal. Place the disc on the mouth of the mug, confetti side up, and carefully press the card down so that it firmly sticks to the top edges with the Blu-tack. Make sure there aren't any noticeable gaps between the disc and the mug. Once it's prepared it should like the mug is full of confetti, not that there's a disc stuck on the top! If any of the Blu-tack shows around the edges, push a couple of loose bits of confetti on to them.

Fill the bowl with confetti and finally bury the sweetie-filled mug deep to one side of the bowl, being careful not to knock off the 'feke'.

Put the scarf into a pocket, or drape it over your table where you can easily grab it.

Performance

Show the audience the big bowl, and tell them how confetti always reminds you of celebrations. Show the empty mug, scoop it into the confetti and take it out, overflowing, being careful not to disturb the secretly prepared mug hidden to one side of the bowl under the confetti. Brush off the excess and pour the confetti back from a height, to make it more dramatic.

Do this once more, making sure you don't reveal the hidden mug. Keep up a patter about celebrations and how there's always something nice to eat at parties.

Now for the tricky bit: plunge the empty mug back into the confetti, but this time let go of it and immediately grab the secret mug. You have to do this switch-over in one flowing movement, so the audience won't suspect anything.

Raise the mug as before (really the secret one), and shake off the excess confetti and say something like, 'It's time for a celebration!' Lift up the scarf with your other hand and place it over the mug, so it completely covers it, and secretly find the edge of the card lid through the material. Say a magic word or make a magic gesture, and whip the scarf away, at the same time pulling the card disc off. Drop the scarf and the lid into the bowl. Pick up the clear plastic bowl and pour the sweets out into it with a flourish. It's a good idea to share them out – then the audience will be sure to like your show!

Le Roy, Talma and Bosco

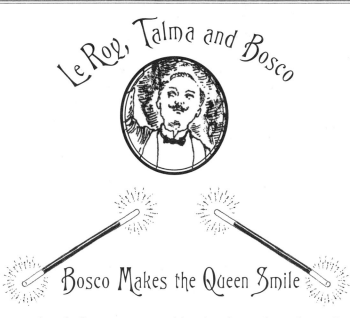

Bosco Makes the Queen Smile

Bosco was a comedian fit for a queen – and here's a funny thing that will make even the most stern-faced monarch grin! This is a great 'impromptu' stunt – that's something you can do anywhere with no preparation – but this one's designed to be seen really close up.

You'll need an ordinary banknote – a £5 or £10 or £20 note.

Explain to your audience that you can make the queen happy or sad.

Take the banknote and fold it carefully as shown in the illustrations. The fold in the middle of the mouth should be the lowest one, so the fold sinks into the note rather than sticking out from it. In origami –that's the art of paper folding – people call this a 'valley fold'.

If you hold the note facing you and then slowly tilt it forward and backwards, the Queen's face does indeed seem to change from a happy expression to a sad one!

Cunning Coin Magic

Le Roy taught Talma to be one of the greatest coin magic acts in the business. Coins are the perfect magic prop, and although Talma performed on the largest stages, coin tricks are ideally suited to small audiences. This branch of magic is still very popular today – because coins are everyday objects that people keep on them all the time (and they're much easier to carry about than floating ladies!). Here are a few more techniques that are a bit trickier than the routine Talma showed us, but they're great fun to learn.

The Vanishing Coin

There are lots of techniques for vanishing a coin into thin air. This one is known as the 'Tourniquet Pass' or 'French Drop' (don't worry – that's not the guillotine). It takes practice to perform really well, but if you learn it properly you'll always be able to amaze people with it. The effect is that you pass a coin from one hand to the other – and it then vanishes into thin air (the coin, that is, not your hand!). And when you've mastered this move, you can use it to vanish any small object – a sweet, say, or a ring.

Fig. 1

A coin is shown between the thumb and the first finger of your right hand, as shown in fig. 1 (although if you're left-handed, you may find it easier to swap the role each hand plays). You then place your left hand over the coin (fig. 2), closing your fingers, apparently removing it and holding it in the closed fingers of your left hand. What you've secretly done, though, is relax your right thumb so that the coin falls into your upturned palm (fig. 3). Act as if the coin actually is in the left hand and gently rub your fingers together as if you're making the coin disintegrate. Slowly open up the hand to reveal that the coin has vanished!

Fig. 2

The secret of success is to practise again and again *really* taking the coin from the hand. Then try and do exactly the same actions but allow the coin to stay behind in the right palm. As the left hand moves away with

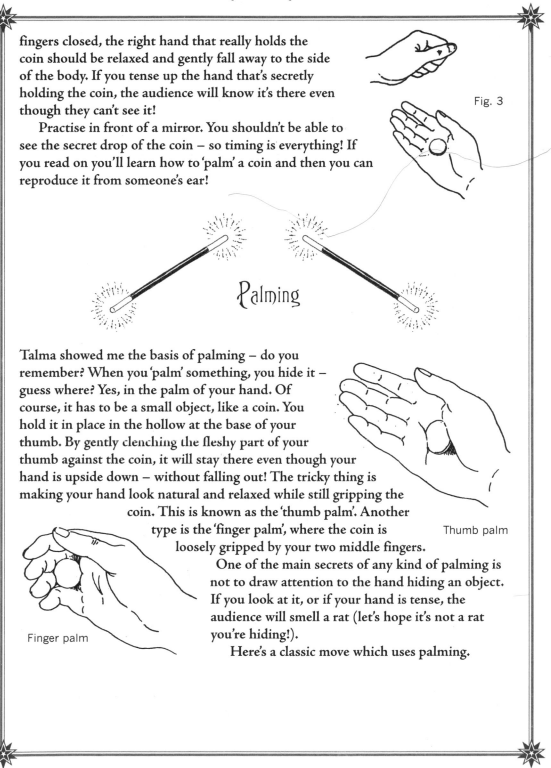

fingers closed, the right hand that really holds the coin should be relaxed and gently fall away to the side of the body. If you tense up the hand that's secretly holding the coin, the audience will know it's there even though they can't see it!

Practise in front of a mirror. You shouldn't be able to see the secret drop of the coin – so timing is everything! If you read on you'll learn how to 'palm' a coin and then you can reproduce it from someone's ear!

Fig. 3

Palming

Talma showed me the basis of palming – do you remember? When you 'palm' something, you hide it – guess where? Yes, in the palm of your hand. Of course, it has to be a small object, like a coin. You hold it in place in the hollow at the base of your thumb. By gently clenching the fleshy part of your thumb against the coin, it will stay there even though your hand is upside down – without falling out! The tricky thing is making your hand look natural and relaxed while still gripping the coin. This is known as the 'thumb palm'. Another type is the 'finger palm', where the coin is loosely gripped by your two middle fingers.

Thumb palm

One of the main secrets of any kind of palming is not to draw attention to the hand hiding an object. If you look at it, or if your hand is tense, the audience will smell a rat (let's hope it's not a rat you're hiding!).

Here's a classic move which uses palming.

Finger palm

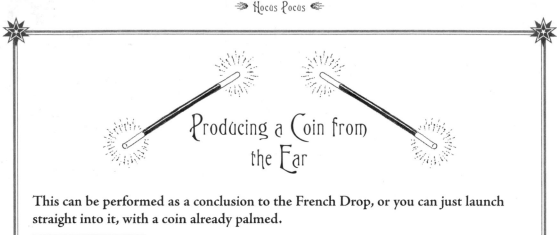

Producing a Coin from the Ear

This can be performed as a conclusion to the French Drop, or you can just launch straight into it, with a coin already palmed.

Start off with the coin in the palmed position, your hand relaxed with the fingers slightly open. Look into the air or to the side of someone's ear. Don't say, 'My hand is empty' or anything like that – your attention should be on the ear! Then reach your hand up as if you've seen something and are going to pick it out. When your hand gets near the ear your thumb quickly slides the palmed coin to the tips of the fingers. Hold the coin still by the side of their head for a moment, so that your audience sees it. With a bit of acting it will look to them as if you've pulled it out of your volunteer's ear!

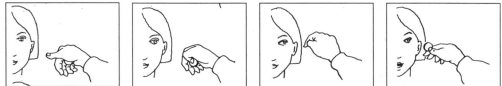

The Coin Roll

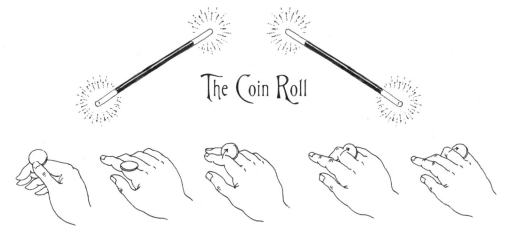

This isn't a trick in itself, but it's a useful 'flourish'. It's very impressive and will keep your fingers well exercised for other sleight-of-hand moves. The illustrations show the move. The idea is that a coin is rolled swiftly over the back of the hand as you pinch it and allow it to roll on to each successive finger, and then pass it back under the palm on the thumb to start again. It's not magic in itself, but it's a great move to add to a magical coin routine and to demonstrate your masterful dexterity!

Robert-Houdin

Remember how Houdin claimed that a scientific phenomenon – the effect of ether – was responsible for the levitation of his son in 'The Ethereal Suspension'? It wasn't, of course. The next magic effect also relies on a scientific principle – or so you tell your audience. It doesn't really (well, not on the one you say it does!!!).

Magnetic Straws

Claiming that you're using the forces of magnetism to move two drinking straws placed on a table, you apparently magnetise your finger by rubbing it against your hair. Placing this finger between the straws causes them to fly apart without even touching them! When somebody else tries, nothing happens – so there must be more magical forces than magnetism at work . . .

Performance

Rubbing your finger in your hair doesn't do anything (apart from mess your hair up) – it's just presentation. You'll need to perform this trick seated at the table with the drinking straws in front of you. It's best not to use bendy straws, but if that's all you have, then carefully snip off the bendy bits with scissors so you're left with perfectly straight straws. The secret is that you blow air from your mouth, quietly and discreetly, at the straws, which causes them to fly apart at great speed!

You'll be surprised at how little air in the right direction will make the straws move in quite an uncanny way. The secret is to fix everyone's attention on the straws and to blow so discreetly than no one notices.

Magic Wand

Robert-Houdin would go nowhere without a magic wand – just about the most famous magician's device of all. The most familiar design is a black rod with a white tip at each end. Ever WANDered why? (Sorry – can't resist it!) There's quite a good reason for it actually: the white tip attracts the spectator's eye, taking attention away from your hand. Also, holding a stick in your hand gives a very good reason to have your hand closed – perfect for concealing the fact that you might have an object hidden there (see page 269). And, of course, when you put down the wand, you can get rid of the palmed object at the same time.

Try it now – see how much more natural it is to palm an object while holding a pen or a stick.

In any case, using a magic wand adds to the air of mystery. It just seems – well, magical! If you want a traditional magic wand you can make your own out of a piece of dowel about 25 cm long and 2 cm in diameter (in case you don't know, dowel is a length of rounded wood). Paint the dowel black, leaving about 4 cm at each end blank. When the black paint is dry, hold the wand in the centre and paint both ends white. It's not a trick in itself – but you can use it during many of your routines, just like Houdin did.

Playing Cards – 52 Ways to Amaze!

Among other accomplishments, Robert-Houdin was a master of sleight of hand with playing cards. So here is a good place to talk a little more about the most popular prop in all of magic.

No wonder so many magic routines involve cards – how else could you hold fifty-two different objects in your hands at the same time? Cards were originally considered to be quite powerful and mysterious things. Tarot cards are still used supposedly to tell people's fortunes. But even ordinary playing cards have interesting connections to the way our planet works. For a start, there are four suits in a pack, like the four seasons in the year. There are thirteen cards in a suit, the same number as there are lunar months. There are fifty-two cards in the pack – the number of weeks in the year. And if you add up every pip on every card, allowing 11 for a jack, 12 for a queen and 13 for a king, and throw in a joker as a 1 for luck (or 2 jokers for a leap year) the total comes to 365 – the number of days in a year. So from this you can see that when cards were first played, they were always seen to have a significance that far outweighed their size.

We've already learned a great card trick from Houdin – so let's look at some techniques, and then learn a few more.

Do the Shuffle!

This sounds simple, but it's essential to get it right. Apart from anything else, shuffling quickly and confidently makes you look like a real magician! If you've ever played cards you may well have seen someone do this – or even tried it yourself. It's not a magical thing in itself, but if you're going to perform card magic you'll need to be able to shuffle a pack of cards!

Turn the page to learn the most common way to mix up a pack of cards. Even if you don't use this for your magic, you'll need this skill every time you play a card game. I'm right-handed so I'll explain it that way around – if you happen to be left-handed (and some of the best magicians are) then just reverse the right and left hands in the directions.

The pictures tell most of the story: start off with the pack in your left hand, backs facing out, with your right hand open and a little below. Now slightly release your grip on the cards with your left hand and use your right thumb to pull off a small stack of cards – around ten or so – into your right hand. Then pull off about another

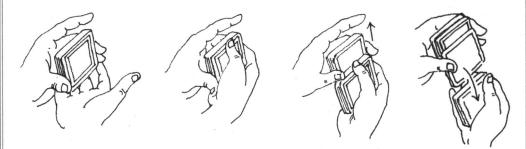

ten or so on to the first stack. Keep pulling off little stacks of cards until the left hand is empty, then place the pack back in the left hand and start over again. Go through the complete pack two or three times quite swiftly, and the result is a pack of cards with the order mixed up randomly. When you get more advanced with your card magic you'll learn secret magic moves based on the overhand shuffle – so it's worth learning to do well.

Squaring Up the Cards

Once you've shuffled the pack, you need to 'square up' the cards. This just means getting the cards to be neatly stacked – you can tap them on a table, first on their short sides and then on their long sides to get the edges exact. Or you can push all the sides together with your fingers as shown. If you do this while the cards are sideways, it is a useful way to secretly glimpse the bottom card of the pack! That'll come in handy very soon.

Cutting the Pack

Cutting the pack doesn't involve a pair of scissors! It's a way of changing the order of the cards, mixing them up into a random order. You simply lift roughly half the pack off the top with one hand, keeping all the cards squared up, and place these to one side. You then pick up the remaining cards and place those on top of the first stack. In this way, a card originally placed on the top ends up lost somewhere in the centre of the pack.

Here are a couple of tricks that depend on cutting the pack – starting with one that's very simple but always proves baffling!

The Mystical Three

The Magic

A volunteer picks a card and memorises it. They place the card back on the top of the pack and 'cut' the pack themselves (see above). You then spread them out and, with some help from a special card, you mysteriously identify the chosen one. And there's an extra surprise at the end.

Preparation

Before the performance, remove the two jokers from the pack, plus one of the threes (it doesn't matter whether it's a heart, a club, a spade or a diamond). With the rest of the pack face down, put the number three card face up at the bottom. Then put the two jokers face down below the number three. Square up the cards and you're ready.

Performance

Explain that you're going to find a chosen card using a mystical number. Spread out the pack of cards in your hands (being careful not to expose the face-up card towards the bottom) and ask a member of the audience to take out a card, face down, look at it and remember it. You place the pack face down on the table and ask your volunteer to place their chosen card face down on top. Ask them to cut the cards, and you neatly square up the pack. (By cutting the cards, the two jokers and the number three card will land directly above the chosen card.)

Concentrating on the pack, and without touching it, you say, 'Do you believe in magical numbers?' You then pick up the pack and spread out the cards from left to right, face down. (If you're left-handed, spreading them right to left will be easier.) One of the cards, a three, is face up, and you say, 'Ah! There it is: the magical number three.' Explain that the number three has always had magical properties – the Ancient Egyptians realised this when they built the pyramids. You then count down three cards from the left of the three (or right, if you spread the cards right to left), without turning them over. Ask your volunteer to name the chosen card. When they do so, you turn over this third card with a flourish – it's the chosen one! Then say, 'Now you may wonder if I was joking about the number three – perhaps you should ask these chaps here,' and you turn over the two face-down cards in between to show that they are the two jokers!

You Do as I Do

This seems truly impossible! It may be the most amazing magical feat for you to learn in the book.

The Magic

Two complete packs of cards are used in this mind-boggling trick. You and a volunteer each choose a card from a different pack. The spectator follows your instructions carefully through a series of shuffles and cuts. At the end the two of you swap packs and find the card you originally chose – incredibly, both cards prove to be the same!

Preparation

There's no preparation required for this. The secret is identifying a 'key' card and making sure the cards are cut in the right way. And check that you have two complete packs – if there are any cards missing this could be disastrous! It's best to remove the jokers.

Performance

Show the audience two packs of cards on the table, and invite a volunteer to sit opposite you and choose one of them.

'Human beings are amazing,' you say, 'and some people believe that we connect in ways that science doesn't always explain. Let's see what happens if we try and get on the same wavelength by synchronising our actions for a couple of minutes. Please do as I do.'

Shuffle your pack of cards thoroughly and deliberately. The best way to do this is the 'overhand shuffle', done slowly, as described earlier. The volunteer does the same. Tell them to keep the timing the same as you both mix the cards up.

As you finish shuffling (here's the secret bit!), tip the pack sideways, and as you square them up in your hand, quickly glimpse the very bottom card (fig. 1). Don't draw attention to this – in fact you can say, 'Make sure the cards are nicely squared up,' as you look, and the spectator will look at their pack at the same time (misdirection!). The card you see will be your 'key' card, so make sure you remember it!

Fig. 1

Tell your spectator, 'So that we are properly in tune with each other, let's swap our packs of cards,' which you then do. Of course, you secretly know the bottom card of the pack they now have.

Ask them to spread their cards in front of them as you do the same (fig. 2), and then allow their fingers to drift over the backs of the cards and come to rest on any one that they want. Ask them to push this card forward, face down, at the same time as you do with your card (it actually doesn't matter which one you pick), again emphasising that everything should be done exactly together (fig. 3). Let's imagine they picked the three of clubs – although you wouldn't know this, of course (not yet, anyway).

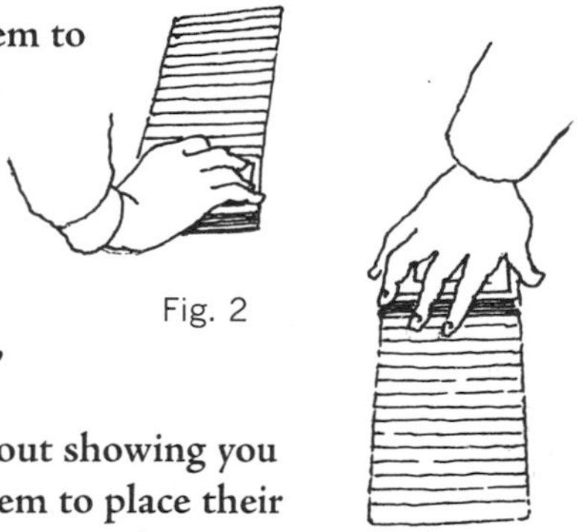

Fig. 2

Ask them to pick the card up and look at it without showing you and, most importantly, to remember it. Then ask them to place their card on the top of the pack, face down, as you do the same. (Although you look at the card you pushed forward, you don't have to remember it – just

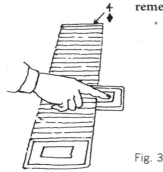

Fig. 3

remember that 'key' card you glimpsed at the start.) You 'square' your cards up on the table and the spectator, copying your moves, does the same. This means their card will be at the top of their pack and your secret 'key' card at the bottom (fig. 4).

Now you ask the spectator to cut their pack as you cut yours ('cutting' the pack was explained on page 274) – placing around half of the cards to one side, and placing the remaining cards on top of them. They won't know this, but this puts the bottom card – your 'key' card – directly above the spectator's chosen card, which they placed on the top of the pack. This will allow you to find it in a few moments. Just to make things more impressive, you and the volunteer cut the cards twice more – the chosen cards are

Fig. 4

well and truly lost. (Make sure the cut is completed each time, and emphasise to them that every move has to be done at the same time as you.)

Tell the audience that neither you nor the volunteer could have the slightest idea where the chosen cards are. You swap packs again (you and the spectator are now holding the packs that you both originally shuffled). Ask the volunteer to look through their pack and find their chosen card, and place it face down on the table. You say that you'll do the same – but in fact you're looking for your 'key' card (fig. 5).

It doesn't matter how many times they have cut the pack, their chosen card will always be the one immediately in front of your 'key' card. (Note: although this is very unlikely, if the 'key' card happens by chance to be the one at the very bottom of the pack, their chosen one will be at the very top.) Take this, actually the spectator's chosen card, and place it face down on the table – it isn't really the one you 'chose' at the same time as the spectator.

Fig. 5

'We've been doing the same moves at the same time – wouldn't it be amazing if somehow we've chosen the same card?' you say, as you both turn over the 'chosen' cards at the same time – and they match!

This piece of magic is reputation-making!

David Devant

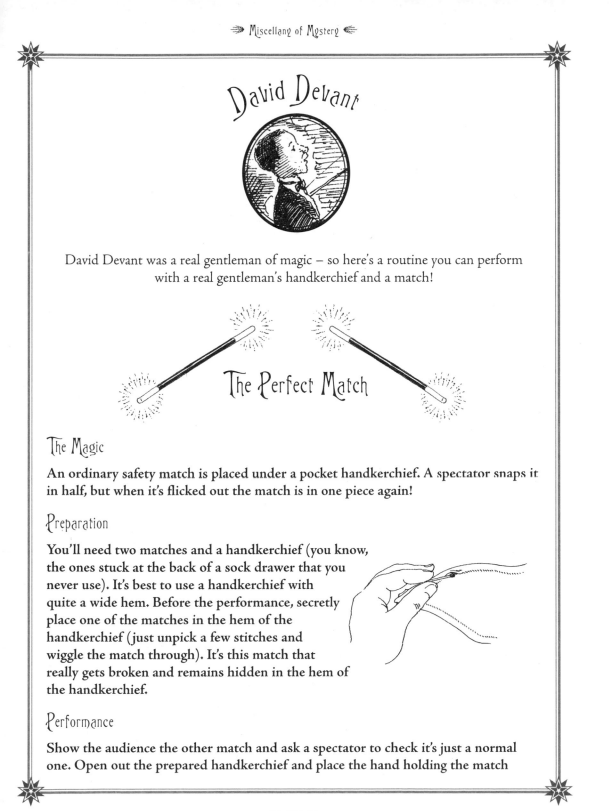

David Devant was a real gentleman of magic — so here's a routine you can perform with a real gentleman's handkerchief and a match!

The Perfect Match

The Magic

An ordinary safety match is placed under a pocket handkerchief. A spectator snaps it in half, but when it's flicked out the match is in one piece again!

Preparation

You'll need two matches and a handkerchief (you know, the ones stuck at the back of a sock drawer that you never use). It's best to use a handkerchief with quite a wide hem. Before the performance, secretly place one of the matches in the hem of the handkerchief (just unpick a few stitches and wiggle the match through). It's this match that really gets broken and remains hidden in the hem of the handkerchief.

Performance

Show the audience the other match and ask a spectator to check it's just a normal one. Open out the prepared handkerchief and place the hand holding the match underneath. As you do so, grab the match that is hidden in the hem and push it up against the middle of the hanky. Ask the spectator to hold it through the cloth, snap it in half and drop it back on your hand. They will never know that the one they are snapping is really the duplicate in the hem.

Once they have released the match, flick the hanky away to show the original match on the palm of your hand. The broken pieces will remain hidden in the hem. It will seem as if the match is restored!

Remote-Control Cards

Devant invented some amazing card magic. Here is something inspired by one of his creations – he actually performed a very similar routine himself, which he described in his book, *Our Magic*.

The Magic

A magical transmitter is used to make a couple of playing cards seemingly travel invisibly from one pack to another.

Preparation

What You Need

* Two packs of cards (they must have identical back designs – you might have to buy new ones)
* A small box, e.g. an empty shoebox
* A TV remote control (the 'transmitter')

If you want the effect to look more magical, you could always make yourself a fancy-looking transmitter out of silver paper and springs. And you should cover the shoebox with some coloured paper.

Put the remote control in the box. Shuffle one of the packs of cards really thoroughly and count twenty-six cards off the top into a pile. Because you've mixed the pack up, it'll be a nice random selection. Place the half-pack that's left over carefully in the box next to the remote control and don't touch these cards until the show.

Now take the other brand-new pack of cards out of its box and find twenty-six cards that match the twenty-six you counted off the first pack (the ones that aren't in the shoebox). Then shuffle this half-pack thoroughly. Put away the cards that are left over – you don't need these at all.

You should now have two identical half-packs in front of you. Place these together, but be careful not to shuffle them again! You will now have a 'pack' of fifty-two cards – really, a set of twenty-six cards followed by twenty-six identical cards in a different order. Place this pack into one of the card boxes, and mark the card box with a little symbol, so you know they are your secretly prepared cards. Put them in your pocket and place the shoebox containing your TV remote control and a half-pack of cards on a table, ready for the show.

Performance

Say to your audience something like, 'Magicians have always used science in their magical experiments. I am going to show you something today which uses an amazing invention – a card-transmitting device! Now, if I could ask someone from the audience to come up and help me . . .'

When someone comes up, sit them on a chair beside you. Show them the special pack of cards and say, 'As you can see, this is a pack of cards.' You don't ask if there are any duplicates of the cards. Of course, the pack actually consists of two sets of the same twenty-six cards – but a spectator won't notice this, especially if you don't draw their attention to it. So don't say, 'Are the cards all different?' You're better off saying something like, 'Are the cards all the same size?'

Square the pack up and then ask your volunteer to count twenty-six cards face down from the top of the pack on to the table. Ask them to hold these counted cards very tightly and make sure that no one can get near them.

Go towards the audience with the remaining cards (really duplicates of the half-pack that the spectator is holding) and fan them out face up so that they can see the different cards. Ask two people to think of 'any card that you can see'. This is important: you have to emphasise that they should remember a card they can actually see, not one that they think of. Once they have done this, square the cards back up neatly and then walk over to the box on your table.

Now comes the only tricky part for you. Explain that you have a special card-transmitting device – a new piece of science! You will still be holding half the pack – the half from which the spectators' cards have just been chosen. Place both your hands into the shoebox and, as you do so, leave behind the half-pack of cards that you were holding and, with the same hand, pick up the half-pack that you secretly placed there earlier. At the same moment pick up the remote control with the other hand. Try to do this without hesitating. You'll find that because you have just explained to the audience about the remote control being in the box, they won't worry about what you're doing – they'll just think that you're picking up the transmitting device.

You will now have the remote in one hand and twenty-six different cards in the other.

All that is left is the presentation. Ask the audience members to concentrate on their chosen cards, point the TV remote control at them, and then point it at the half-pack in your hands. Then explain that you will beam the cards over to the first volunteer. After a few moments of concentration, ask the spectators for the first time to name their chosen cards out loud. Put down the transmitter and fan the cards out in your hands. Their chosen cards will not be in there – you know this because, really, the cards they looked at earlier are now hidden in the shoebox. You are holding a different half-pack (remember the sneaky switch you did as you picked up the TV remote?).

Ask your first volunteer to fan through their cards and, amazingly, the chosen cards have arrived. (This half of the pack has all the same cards as those the spectators looked at.)

Make sure you thank your helpers and take a bow for a great piece of magic!

Chung Ling Soo

Here are a couple of curious pieces of magic inspired by Chung Ling Soo's visit.

Banana Split

While Soo showed us scissors that don't cut, here's an opposite feat! It's really a puzzle, but try it out!

The Magic

You take an ordinary banana, and, after some amusing magical gestures, show that somehow it has been cut into slices while its skin is in one piece!

Preparation

All you need is a banana and a wooden cocktail stick. The secret is in the way you prepare the banana.

Put the banana on a placemat, and then carefully push the cocktail stick through one point of the banana skin and slide it from side to side (as shown in the illustration over the page).

The cocktail stick will slice through the banana, but be careful not to push it through the skin on the other side (or your finger!). Make sure that you never put your hand under the banana directly opposite the stick – just steady it at one end. Move the stick a little further down the same 'ridge' of the banana, and once again move it back and forth, cutting through the banana. Do this five or six times.

Your banana is prepared. Try to do this just before your show, otherwise the banana will go horribly brown. The best bananas to use are those with slightly spotty skins, as they're less likely to show the marks left by the cocktail stick. (But don't use very ripe bananas – the bits will stick together.)

Performance

Show the banana and ask someone to check that it's intact – it's not been peeled at all. Draw the audience's attention to the ends of the banana more than the middle.

All that is left is presentation. You could explain to the audience that you've learned an ancient form of martial arts that allows you to cut through things in an impossible way. You hold the banana out and make karate-style slicing actions with your right hand above it, all the way along (complete with sound effects – 'Hiiii–Ya!').

When you peel open the banana, it's been magically sliced into lots of pieces!

Sun and Moon

Some of Soo's routines involved objects and people mysteriously switching places. Here's a simple routine where two pictures drawn on paper seem to swap places!

The Magic

You take two pieces of paper, each about the size of a £10 note. On one you draw a picture of the sun, the other the moon. You place the moon drawing on top of the sun and roll them up together around a pencil. When you unroll them, the moon is under the sun – you've changed night into day!

Preparation and Performance

Not much preparation to do – just make sure you have the two pieces of paper and a pen to draw with (and roll the paper around). Once you've drawn the sun and moon on the two pieces of paper, lay the 'sun' paper on the table so that the short end is nearest to you, and place the 'moon' paper square on top but about 1 cm further away. Place a pencil across the short side of the paper nearest to you and start rolling them up together, telling the audience that in ancient times people believed that magicians could change day into night.

Because the top paper (with the moon drawn on it) is slightly further away than the other, as you roll slowly, at a certain point one end of the lower 'sun' piece of paper will flick around the pencil and land on top. This is the secret move and you should use your fingers to conceal the end as it flips around the pencil (together with a bit of 'misdirection') so that your spectators don't see it happen. As soon as this happens, stop and ask the spectator to put their fingers on the end of the papers, so they can't move. Most of the paper will still be rolled around the pencil, but they'll still be able to trap the two ends on to the table top. Unbeknown to them the pieces have already swapped – but this isn't revealed until you unroll the paper. This trick works almost by itself – just try it by following the illustrations carefully.

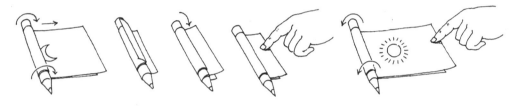

Ionia

The first magic effect Ionia inspired is the one that her mother, Okita, was famous for – the 'Linking Rings', one of the most well-known stage magic routines of all time. Thousands of magicians have performed variations on this theme throughout the past hundred years or so. I recommend that one day you go to a magic shop and ask for a good set of professional linking rings and study them all you can. They really are a wonderful piece of magic – and were one of the first proper magic tricks I ever learned. Meanwhile, I don't suppose you have a set of rings knocking around now, so I'll show you a simpler, quicker trick with the same theme.

Linking Paper Clips

This is really a bit of fun, not something to make a big mystery out of – but you'll fool yourself and others if you try it! All you need is a banknote, two paper clips and an elastic band.

Performance

Hold the banknote horizontally and fold about a third of the banknote across itself, then push a paper clip on to the top about halfway along the fold. Then slip a rubber band on to the middle of the note. Finally, fold the back side of the note inwards in the opposite direction and place another paper clip on the note. Both paper clips should be on the top edge of the folded note as shown in the illustrations.

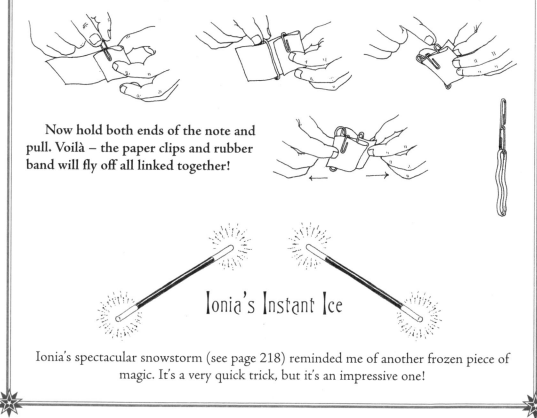

Now hold both ends of the note and pull. Voilà – the paper clips and rubber band will fly off all linked together!

Ionia's Instant Ice

Ionia's spectacular snowstorm (see page 218) reminded me of another frozen piece of magic. It's a very quick trick, but it's an impressive one!

The Magic

The magician seems to change water into ice with a touch of their hand!

Preparation

Find a mug (not a transparent one), four sheets of good quality (thick) kitchen towel and an ice cube.

   Fold up the kitchen towel neatly and press it into the bottom of the mug. Place an ice cube on top of the paper just before doing the trick.

Performance

Explain to your audience that you've learned how to freeze water with just a touch of your hand. Take the prepared mug and tip in a little water – just enough so that it all gets absorbed by the kitchen towel. After waiting a couple of seconds, tip the mug upside down – the ice cube will fall out, but the soaked kitchen paper will stay in the bottom of the mug (provided you don't shake it too much).

   If you're performing this in the middle of a show, you could either find a plastic ice cube from a joke shop, or change the water into something else – like a blue bouncy ball. Be sure to practise to get the quantity of water right – you don't want to get it wrong and tip water on the floor. That would certainly lead to a frosty reception!

Sugar-Symbol Sorcery

   Ionia, along with many other magicians of the Golden Age, drew on the fascinating culture of Ancient Egypt to add an air of mystery to her shows. Her mummy case and other apparatus would all have been decorated with colourful Egyptian symbols – hieroglyphics. This close-up illusion is a very mysterious piece of magic involving a vanishing and reappearing symbol . . .

The Magic

Using a pencil, the spectator draws a shape on the side of a sugar cube, which you then drop into a glass of warm water. The sugar dissolves – but the symbol magically appears on the spectator's hand!

Preparation

All you need for this piece of magic is a clear glass of warm water, a soft pencil (like a 2B – though if you have only an HB, that would do too), a white sugar cube and a teaspoon (or a magic wand).

Performance

This excellent close-up illusion has an interesting secret: you make an impression of the symbol on your thumb and transfer it to your spectator's hand without them noticing!

You set the scene by talking about how the Ancient Egyptians communicated through the use of symbols and pictures. Ask a spectator to write a simple, clear shape on one whole side of the sugar cube – something like a star, square or triangle. Ask them to draw as large as they can fit on to the side of the cube, and to make the drawing as clear as possible.

While they are drawing the symbol, secretly lick your thumb so that it is slightly wet (not soaked!). Then, when you take the cube back, point to the glass of water and at the same time press your thumb firmly against the drawing on the side of the cube. This transfers the pencil mark on to your thumb.

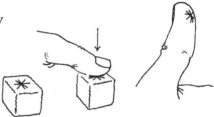

Drop the sugar into the glass and stir it with the teaspoon or wand until it dissolves – being careful not to use the hand with the imprinted thumb! Meanwhile, chat more about mystical Egyptian magic: 'The symbol has now disappeared – vanished into the water never to be seen again. But in Ancient Egypt they believed that the dead would live again – that's why they were buried with all their treasure! So let's see if the same thing will happen to your symbol . . .' Your expression turns to one of great concentration.

Next, ask the spectator to lift their hand upwards, palm down. Pull their hand slightly towards you and place it on top of the glass of water. As you do so, firmly press your thumb against their face-down palm. This will transfer the pencil mark on to the underside of their hand. As you perform this 'secret' move, make sure that your actions are matched with appropriate chat – say something like, 'Just rest your hand over the glass like this,' and fix your audience's attention on to the dissolved sugar in the glass. This will 'misdirect' the audience from the secret move.

Afterwards, your spectator won't even remember that you have touched their hand, because their attention was so fixed on the dissolved sugar cube!

All that remains is a bit of presentation. Chant something mystical like, 'Hocus Pocus' and ask the spectator to slowly turn their hand over. To their astonishment the symbol will seem to have risen out of the water and printed itself on their hand!

Houdini

Houdini issued challenges wherever he went. Here are a few simple ones that seem impossible – unless you know how. Great fun for you and your friends to try.

The Rope Challenge

Tell your friends you can tie a knot in a piece of rope without letting go of the ends. They'll try and try but won't be able to do it – but you can do it in an instant!

You'll need a piece of rope or thick string about 30 cm long. Rest it on a table in front of you. Now fold your arms and grab hold of the two ends of the rope, one end at a time. This is a bit tricky but try it a couple of times and it will work. Once you have a firm hold of the ends simply unfold your arms. A knot will appear in the centre of the rope!

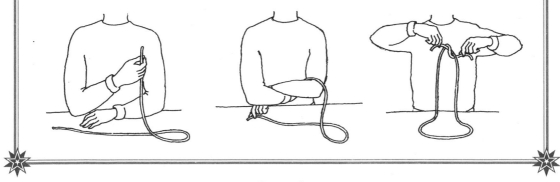

The Great Rubber-Band Escape

You place an elastic band round two of your fingers and trap it in place by wrapping another band around all of your fingertips. You then tell your spectators that it will escape from the two fingers – and it instantly appears on the other two!

 With the back of your hand facing the audience, place a rubber band on your third and fourth fingers, and interlock a second rubber band over all your fingers as shown, trapping the first band. Now, stretching the first band out with the other hand, fold your fingers over, as shown in the illustrations. Insert the ends of all four fingers into the rubber band – and let go with the other hand. Then, after a

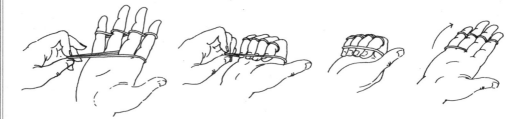

moment's pause, straighten up your fingers. The first band will automatically jump from two fingers over to the other two as if by magic! If you practise in front of a mirror, you'll find there's a way of stretching the first rubber band just enough to get your fingers into, but not so much that the audience can see your secret move.

The Great Mint Escape

All you need are eight Polo mints (the ones with the hole!), a long piece of string and a large handkerchief.

The Magic

A pile of Polo mints threaded on a string magically penetrates through a single mint!

Performance

It's best to perform this routine close up above a table top. Explain to your audience that sweets can behave a bit oddly, and you are going to show them what you mean.

Thread the first mint on to the string as if you were threading a bead on to a necklace (fig. 1). Then hold the two ends of the string together and thread six mints on to this double length of string one at a time. They will all sit on top of the first Polo mint and won't fall off – they can't (fig. 2)!

Fig. 1

Fig. 2

Here's the secret move. Thread the eighth mint on to only one of the strings, and it will sit on top of the other six mints balanced on the single one at the bottom (fig. 3). The audience should not be aware that this eighth mint has gone on any differently to the preceding six.

Fig. 3

Ask a spectator to hold both ends of the string while you cover their hand and the mints with the handkerchief. Emphasise that it would be impossible to remove the mints from the string as they are trapped on at one end by a sideways mint, and held by the spectator at the other. Reach underneath to the bottom mint – the one you first threaded on to the string. Grab it with both hands and snap it in half (fig. 4). You'll need to provide some misdirection here – keep chatting to your audience in a relaxed way, even though it might be a bit tricky to snap the mint, and hide the pieces in your hand.

As soon as you've done this, all the other mints will fall off the string – they'll seem to have magically passed through the other one. Remove the handkerchief and there will still be one mint threaded on the string (fig. 5). The audience will imagine it was the one you threaded on right at the beginning of the challenge, but it's really the last one you secretly threaded on to the single piece of string.

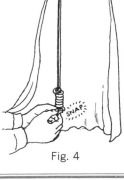

Fig. 4

Fig. 5

The Grand Illusion

This is where the magic gets BIG! Houdini vanished an elephant and spent his career performing amazing big scale stunts and illusions. Well, making an elephant disappear isn't too practical these days – so why not make a friend or brother or sister appear from nowhere? They're much easier to train up than an elephant (and they eat less). This was invented by a very clever man known as 'General' U. F. Grant – he invented hundreds of mysteries!

The Magic

You show the audience two cardboard boxes, with their tops and bottoms removed. They are both entirely empty and can be folded flat. When they're opened up, one box is put over the other – and your assistant jumps out as if from nowhere!!

Preparation

Apart from two willing assistants, the two boxes are all you need – but one of them is secretly altered and slightly smaller than the other. The boxes that computers come in would be useful here (with their tops and bottoms cut off), or you could make your own out of corrugated cardboard or even hardboard, sticking the sides together with heavy-duty parcel tape.

It's the smaller box that holds the secret – the opening cut into it on one side (see fig. 1). This must be hidden from the audience at all times.

By the time you're ready to perform, you and your assistants will be on the stage (or at one end of your room with no spectators behind you), along with the two boxes. The boxes are folded flat and standing upright – your first assistant will have to steady them. The smaller box is in front, with its secret opening facing back. Your second assistant, the one who's going to 'appear', is crouching behind the two boxes, out of sight of the audience.

Fig. 1

Performance

You start by indicating the flattened boxes to the audience. Then you lift up the smaller box and show it in its flattened state, making sure that the spectators can see how thin it is and that therefore it couldn't conceal anything (and being careful not to show them the side with the big hole cut in it – see fig. 2). Place it back on the floor and open it out (keeping the secret opening at the back) so that it overlaps the left edge of the other box. Your second assistant quietly crawls from behind the box that's still being held by the first assistant and into the box in front, through the secret opening (fig. 3).

Fig. 2

All this time you should be talking to the audience, spinning a story of some kind. Or you could present this to music as a dramatic finale to your show.

Next, you lift up the larger box and open it out, showing the audience that it is absolutely empty. With one easy flowing movement, you place this box over the other one (fig. 4).

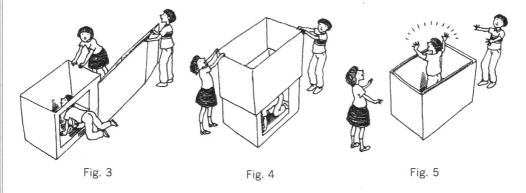

Fig. 3

Fig. 4

Fig. 5

Now for your magic spell: clap your hands and the hidden assistant suddenly jumps up out of the box and out of the blue (fig. 5)!

> The prediction for It's Mentally Mathemagical
>
> is 1089. Now go back to page 261 …

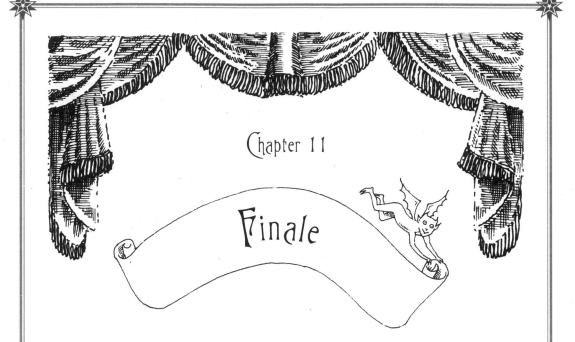

Chapter 11

Finale

J ust like the great magicians, there will come a time when, if you've learned how to do some magic really well, you'll want to put on your own show. Here are a few things for you to think about before your performance.

Prop Table

You'll have realised by now that many magic routines depend on carefully prepared props, and if you're doing a show you'll have to work out where to put them. You don't want to risk showing up for a performance and not being able to find the right table – so it may well be worth considering finding something you can take with you. A trolley is ideal because you can set up all the props in one room and then wheel them into another room without disturbing them too much. If you use the lower shelf of the trolley to store your props, you can use the top as a working surface during the show. You could even get a fancy cloth and hang it over the front so that no one can see the props set up behind.

Costume

Think about what you might wear for your show. Do you want to look traditional – smart with a suit and a bow tie? Or perhaps you can find an old tail jacket from a charity or fancy-dress shop and look like Robert-Houdin? There are lots of magicians today who dress very casually, in normal street clothes. This all depends on what kind of magician you want to be – mysterious or funny, chatty or silent, traditional or modern.

Styles of performance

As you've seen from all the magicians you've met in the book, they all have different ways of presenting their magic. Alexander was a serious mind-reader, Soo was a silent mysterious character, Bosco was a clown, Houdini was a challenging sensation-maker!

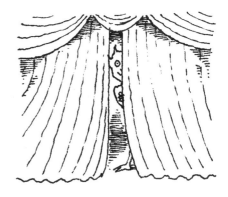

Think about what sort of magician you would most like to be. The best way of deciding is to try out lots of different styles when you start out. See which one you get most enjoyment out of, and which one gets the most positive response from your audiences.

Where to perform

Many people first try out their magic on their family and friends. You'll soon find that once people know that you can do a few tricks you'll be asked to perform at unexpected times – so if you don't want to disappoint, always try to have something on you so that you can do magic whenever you're asked! That's one reason why card magic is so popular – it's easier to carry a pack of cards on you than a vanishing elephant! That's also what's great about knowing things that rely on pure skill, such as the 'French Drop' coin vanish (see page 268) – you'll always be able to perform it with any small object!

If you get really good and develop a routine, you might want to try doing a show at a local old people's home or day centre – they're often looking for entertainment. That's how I started out doing shows! If you do take on any performing jobs away from family and friends, make sure that you're reliable and practise extra hard! The other place you might be able to try out your magic is at school – ask your form teacher if you can perform some magic at the end of term in front of your class, or maybe in assembly!

Music

Think about using music in your shows – it can be a great way to add atmosphere! You can find some music on a CD and play it from a portable stereo system. Some people perform their whole acts to music.

Routining – the order of tricks

Think about the order that you might perform a series of tricks. You could start off with something impressive and quick (like 'Ionia's Instant Ice', page 286) and end with something spectacular (like 'Sweet Confetti', page 264). The choice of magic you perform should depend on the size of audience too. If you're seated around a dinner table you can use much smaller props and effects than if you were in a large hall. Try to vary the effects in your show – it's not great to do all card tricks, for example, although you can get away with more than one if they are very different (for instance, 'The Electric Telegraph' card trick is about cards being transmitted through the air, whereas Houdin's 'Invisible Card' trick is about a card becoming – yes – invisible). A possible routine for a small audience might be:

☞ Vanishing a coin and reproducing it from someone's ear (p. 268 and p. 270)
☞ Talma's Travelling Coins (p. 104)
☞ The Perfect Match (p. 279)
☞ You Do as I Do (p. 276)

A possible routine for a larger audience based on the tricks in this book could be:

☞ Houdin's Invisible Card (p. 131)
☞ Reading between the Lines (p. 261)
☞ An Ionian Snowstorm (p. 214)

✺

So, as we draw to a close, try to remember the lessons you've learned from some of these masters of magic. Remember the mystery in magic, make sure that you concentrate on sharing something fantastic with your audience and practise before you perform so that your magic looks as good as you can make it. Keep the secrets too: telling people how it's done is usually disappointing to them. But the most important thing: enjoy what you're doing – that way the audience will enjoy it too. Magic is a wonderful world, an international language, and once you're hooked and get really good at it, it's something that can introduce you to people you'd never have otherwise met, take you to places you've never dreamed of going and give you pleasure throughout your life.

It's time for me to disappear.

Bibliography

Altick, Richard D., *The Shows of London* (Harvard, MA, 1978)

Alexander, C., *The Life and Mysteries of the Celebrated Dr Q* (Ohio, 1946)

Andrews, Val, *A Gift from the Gods* (Bromsgrove, Worcestershire, 1981)

Beckmann, Darryl, *The Life and Times of Alexander* (Washington, 1994)

Burrows, J. F., *Programmes of Magicians* (London, 1906)

Caveney, Mike, and William Rauscher, *Servais Le Roy: Monarch of Mystery* (Pasadena, CA, 1999)

Charvet, David, *Alexander: The Man Who Knows* (Pasadena, CA, 2004)

Christopher, Milbourne, *Illustrated History of Magic* (London, 1975)

Clarke, Sidney W., *Annals of Conjuring* (New York, 1983)

Davenport, Anne, and John Salisse, *St George's Hall* (Pasadena, CA, 2001)

Dawes, Edwin A., *The Great Illusionists* (London, 1979)

Devant, David, *My Magic Life* (London, 1931)

Devant, David, *Secrets of My Magic* (London, 1936)

Dexter, Will, *The Riddle of Chung Ling Soo* (London, 1955)

Fechner, Christian, *The Magic of Robert Houdin: An Artist's Life* (Boulogne, France, 2002)

Gaughan, John, and Jim Steinmeyer, *Antonio Diavolo: A Souvenir of his Performance* (Los Angeles, 1986)

Hackney Gazette, 1900–1920

Hibberd, David, *Chronicle of Magic 1900–1999* (Exmouth, Devon, 2003)

Hoffmann, Professsor (Angelo Lewis), *Modern Magic* (London, 1876)

Hoffmann, Professsor (Angelo Lewis), *Tips for Tricyclists* (London, 1888)

Houdini, Harry, *A Magician among the Spirits* (New York, 1924)

Jennes, George A., *Maskelyne and Cooke* (Enfield, Middlesex, 1967)

Lafayette fire story, *Edinburgh Evening News* (Edinburgh, May 1911)

Le Roy's letters to Percy Naldrett (author's collection)

Lead, Brian, *Lafayette: The Final Act* (Lancashire, c. 1990)

Maskelyne, Nevil, and David Devant, *Our Magic* (London, 1911)

Newmann, C. A. George, *The Collected Mental Secrets of C. A. George Newmann*, ed. by Leo Behnke (South Pasadena, CA, 1990)

Price, David, *Magic: An Illustrated History of Conjurers in the Theatre* (New Jersey, 1985)

'The Queen of Coins' article, *New Penny Magazine*, no 96, vol viii (c. 1910)

Reynolds, Charles and Regina, *100 Years of Magic Posters* (London, 1976)

Robert-Houdin, Jean, *Secrets of Conjuring and Magic*, translated by Professor Hoffmann (London, 1878)

Robert-Houdin, Jean, *Memoirs of Robert-Houdin* (London, 1859)

Sharpe, Sam, *Devant's Delightful Delusions* (Pasadena, CA, 1990)

Sharpe, Sam, *The Magic Play* (Chicago, IL, 1976)

Silverman, Kenneth, *Houdini!!!* (New York, 1996)

Stanyon, Ellis, *Magic* magazine, 1900–1920 (Washington DC, 1996)

Steinmeyer, Jim, *The Glorious Deception* (New York, 2005)

Steinmeyer, Jim, *Hiding the Elephant* (New York, 2003)

Sterling, Max, *The Magical World* magazine (c. 1910–11)

Wilson, Mark, *Mark Wilson's Complete Course in Magic* (Philadelphia, PA, 1998)

Acknowledgements

Special thanks to Christine King, my key badgerer, editor and companion through the first writing stage – I couldn't have done it without you. Your quibbles were always pertinent and helpful! To Sheila Ableman, my literary agent, for incredible enthusiasm, just the right amount of pestering and having faith in the idea in the first place. To Elinor Bagenal for invaluable insight and for rolling the ball in an ambitious direction, Emma Matthewson for commissioning *Hocus Pocus*, Helen Szirtes, my editor at Bloomsbury, for delightful diligence and for magically changing the manuscript into a book. To Peter Bailey and Val Brathwaite for transforming the words into pictures and all at Bloomsbury for more enthusiasm than I could have ever wished for. Special thanks also to Daniel, Marcia and Alan Radcliffe – the idea for this book was born in Daniel's enthusiasm for the subject. To my brothers, Daniel and Mark, sister-in-law Tracey, niece Hannah (who at six is already quite a wizard) and nephew Elliot (who, at two, has already acted as her assistant). To David Jameson for support, cups of tea and for putting up with the magic posters. Early readers Catrin Richards, the Diamond family, Sharron Eglash (a great cousin and an inspiring human being), to my theatrical agent, Rachel Daniels. To Norm and Lupe Neilson for providing poster images, Derren Brown and David Copperfield for their kind words. Thanks to David Hibberd and Peter Lane at The Magic Circle Library. To Simon Thomsett, Othman and Brian at the Hackney Empire (do go and see something there – it's a magical place). To Charles Green for information on Ionia, John Davenport for the legs optical illusion and to Mike Caveney (www.mcmagicwords.com) for his invaluable series of magic profile books. Most of all to my mum, Millie, for encouragement and incredible support throughout my life and late father, Jeff, for inspiring me with his love of history and collecting and for giving up endless football matches to allow me to watch magic videos on the TV in my teens. And not forgetting my dear late sister, Karen, my number one supporter and assistant, to whom this book is dedicated.

A Note on the Acts in Hocus Pocus

Most of the magic acts that take place in the course of the story were actually performed by those magicians during the golden age of magic and are described here with the occasional use of artistic licence. Many of them appeared several times at the Hackney Empire, including: Chung Ling Soo (week of 26 December 1910), Le Roy, Talma and Bosco (week of 17 June 1912), Houdini (week of 8 May 1911), The Great Lafayette (week of 15 February 1911 – just three months before the terrible fire) and David Devant (week of 12 October 1914). Magicians were a regular feature on the stage of the Hackney Empire right up to the end of the variety era in 1956. The new management of the Empire are gradually reintroducing variety back on to their historic stage – so get practising now and you could perform there one day!

For further information about the magicians featured in this book, please visit **www.bloomsbury.com/hocuspocus** and discover many more magical delights. And visit Paul Kieve's website at **www.stageillusion.com**.